THE RESCUE
—— of the ——
Officer Moreland Lee

David Estes

Copyright © 2021 by David Estes

All rights reserved. No part of this publication may be reproduced, distributed, or transmitted in any form or by any means, including photocopying, recording, or other electronic or mechanical methods, without the prior written permission of the publisher, except in the case brief quotations embodied in critical reviews and other noncommercial uses permitted by copyright law.

ISBN: 978-1-63945-045-9 (Paperback)
       978-1-63945-046-6 (Hardback)

The views expressed in this book are solely those of the author and do not necessarily reflect the views of the publisher, and the publisher hereby disclaims any responsibility for them.

Writers' Branding
1800-608-6550
www.writersbranding.com
orders@writersbranding.com

Contents

Chapter 1	The Losers	1
Chapter 2	The Stop	33
Chapter 3	The Phone Call	36
Chapter 4	The Discovery	38
Chapter 5	Alice	40
Chapter 6	Sergeant Miles	43
Chapter 7	The Raid	47
Chapter 8	Maria	51
Chapter 9	The Search	56
Chapter 10	The Security guard	66
Chapter 11	Sarah and Melissa	71
Chapter 12	The Old Man on the Mountain	74
Chapter 13	The Sighting	78
Chapter 14	Posse	83
Chapter 15	The Final Stand	86
Chapter 16	The Reunion	89

CHAPTER I

The Losers

Larry Oliver had had a lousy day. He started his day out by having to beat the crap out of a junkie who had stolen some crack from him. That wasn't an easy task. The offender had failed to report his earnings to Larry then disappeared. Larry had to track him to a vacant home frequented by other addicts. The place was literally a sewer pit. There was no electricity or running water. Someone had cut a hole in the floor so you could urinate or defecate through the hole so the waste would fall into the basement. Larry had gotten lucky. A friendly drug user who needed a fix told Larry where the miscreant could be found. Larry rewarded the junkie with a small rock of crack.

Before going to look for the addict named "D", he decided to pick up his sidekick and business partner named Jeff Moore. He had met Jeff in prison. Larry was in for drug sales and auto theft. Jeff was in prison for strong arm robbery and drug possession. Jeff had decided to snatch a purse from an old lady walking out of a grocery store. He had the misfortune of snatching the purse just as a police cruiser pulled into the lot on a shoplift call.

Both Larry and Jeff came from dysfunctional families. Larry had a father who was a drunk. His father usually spent the money his mother earned cleaning homes on alcohol. Larry's father would beat him when he felt like it and usually for no reason. Larry had learned early to dodge impending violence and punishment. He hated his father and hoped to see him dead.

When he was fifteen he got his wish. His father's liver gave out. At the funeral, Larry didn't say a word out of respect for his mother. Had he spoken, he would have simply told the small gathering of relatives how glad he was that his father was dead, and what a despicable person he was.

Larry began his criminal career when he was fourteen. Shoplifting became a way of life for him. He loved the excitement of stealing items without getting caught. By the time he was sixteen, he was an old hand at stealing. Larry began to steal larger more expensive items. Finally, he began to steal wallets and purses. Credit cards became a source of revenue. One time, he took a purse and found a cell phone in it. He found the email info for his victim's spouse. Larry sent him a text asking him for his bank code. The spouse sent him the info without thinking to check the message out. Larry went to a nearby ATM and emptied out his victim's account.

Larry found his cell phone scam worked so well that he decided to use it often. Larry did not pay attention to the surveillance cameras recording his misdeeds. It wasn't long before he showed his friends how easy it was to get money. At one of the ATMs, one of his friends stood with him while he withdrew money. The camera recorded both of them. An astute juvenile detective recognized the friend. Larry's friend was busted. He ratted on Larry to get a better deal. Larry was charged and convicted. Since he was still a juvenile, Larry was given some detention in juvenile hall and let go.

During his incarceration, Larry was introduced to drug sales. When he got out of juvenile, he started to sell drugs obtained from a local dealer who was happy to have Larry sell his drugs.

By the time he was nineteen, Larry was a successful drug supplier. He had several street junkies working for him. Slowly, Larry started to cater to the higher class clientele so he could avoid street junkies and risk detection by the police.

Larry had not totally divested himself from street dealers he employed. One of them got caught by the police. True to form, the street dealer turned snitch and got Larry busted. Another problem Larry had was the stolen car parked in his garage. He got a ten year sentence for drug sales and auto theft. His attorney struck a plea bargain and got the sales reduced to possession and the two offenses to run concurrently. Larry would be out within three years. It was while in prison he met Jeff Moore.

Jeff wasn't abused in his earlier years. He came from over indulgent parents who just didn't care. No matter what Jeff did his parents would just excuse it or ignore it. After a while, Jeff's father would get drunk and beat his mother. When Jeff got old enough, he began resisting his father. That was a mistake at first. Jeff's father would beat Jeff as well. After a couple of years, Jeff got smarter. He finally picked up a baseball bat and struck back one night when his father began beating his mother. Jeff put his father in the hospital for a few days. When Jeff's father got out of the hospital he became quiet and withdrawn. If he got upset at his family, Jeff's father would just walk out of the house. He was very aware that his son kept the bat close by.

Jeff's new found freedom from his father meant that there were even fewer restraints on his activities. It wasn't planned that way, it just happened as a consequence of his confrontation with his father. Jeff soon began to do as he pleased without any interference from his parents.

It wasn't long before Jeff encountered the law. To him, the law was an abstract thing.

Sure he had seen police officers in their cars driving around and saw TV shows but to him police officers were not a factor in his life. To Jeff, police officers were pretty much not around when he would commit his petty crimes. He became adept at shoplifting and purse snatching. When he would snatch a purse, he would plan his escape route and method of stealing carefully. His victims would be elderly women or women who left their purses in a shopping cart. One of his favorite methods was to take a purse out of a shopping bag as the victim walked along the street.

Jeff learned to be careful after a while. Stores began to install video cameras for security reasons. He not only had to plan out his route but to watch for those damn cameras spying on him.

He would usually steal purses around the first of the month or on Fridays. The first of the month meant welfare checks were in. On Fridays it was payday. As far as he was concerned Friday was his payday. Quite often he would select a victim coming out of a bank. Whatever victim he would choose, he would follow the victim until she was ready to get into her car or when she would get off a bus with her groceries.

He did well until he slipped up one day. He snatched a purse just as the victim's son came up in his car to pick up his mother. The son chased him down and held him for the police.

Jeff got his first lesson in juvenile justice. He was put on probation and told to do community service. He had stolen hundreds of dollars. For his efforts, he was sentenced to wash dishes in an old folks home for a month. It wasn't a real surprise when Jeff turned eighteen, and got caught breaking into a business. He was put on probation and made to pay for the broken window. Jeff figured this was business as usual.

Jeff decided to sell drugs to make a living. It was easier to sell drugs than work a normal job. Besides Jeff did not have any work experience or a trade with which to make a living. One day, Jeff was walking out of a grocery store behind an old lady who had just paid cash for some groceries. He was high on his own drugs as usual. The temptation was too great. Instead of planning the snatch, he just went for it without any prior planning. Jeff grabbed the purse then took off running. He looked back to see if anyone was following. Just as he did, he ran into a car in the parking lot. Officers Dunn and Metz of the Seattle Police were stunned to watch a person with a purse run into their police car and bounce off. Needless to say, Jeff, was apprehended on the spot. This time, Jeff, wasn't so lucky. He had broken the old lady's arm when he snatched the purse. Through a public defender, he tried to claim he was innocent which only infuriated the judge for wasting his time with such a cut and dried case. Earlier that morning, the judge had been served with divorce papers and was in no mood for the likes of Jeff. When the judge found out Jeff had broken the woman's arm his disposition got even more sour. Jeff got ten years. With good behavior, he would be out in about four years.

Larry and Jeff hooked up in a weight lifting room in the prison. Both had recognized early on that you either were a punk or you learned how to take care of yourself. Lifting weights was a start. It wasn't long before Larry and Jeff were recognized as strong weight lifters. They became inseparable. When they were out in the yard for exercise, each would have the other's back. A couple of the inmates tried to take the two on. That was a losing proposition. If one was attacked the other jumped in to help out. They soon became known as the "Dynamic Duo".

One time, while in the yard a black gang tried to take Larry and Jeff on all at once. Larry and Jeff backed themselves into a small alcove and fought the group off. After that, word got around to leave the two alone or pay the price.

In the criminal society, "strength" is the main judge of who would be top dog and respected. Larry and Jeff capitalized on this respect from other inmates. It wasn't long before Larry and Jeff had a following. Larry organized his following into an efficient group. Larry made contact with an old acquaintance on the outside that could supply narcotics and other contraband. Jeff made friends with a couple of guards who would look the other way for a price. By the end of their terms, Larry and Jeff had a small but efficient operation supplying the needs of a willing prison population.

Larry and Jeff only had one challenge to their prison operation. A guy named the enforcer got put into prison on assault and attempted murder. The enforcer was a white supremacist who was just mean, ugly and big. One person tried to call him "refrigerator" one time because he was so big. The enforcer took that as a sign of disrespect and promptly broke the guy's arms.

The enforcer was arrested and convicted of trying to kill a police snitch. The enforcer took a baseball bat and broke both of the snitch's legs. He then tied the snitch to a school fence and repeatedly backed into him with a car until almost every bone in his body was broken. At the hospital, the doctors put the guy into a hammock and gave him what little care they could. All felt the snitch would die so no effort was made to try and put him together. Incredibly the snitch survived the night. Doctors then began to put him back together again. To their surprise and to the chagrin of the enforcer the snitch lived to testify against the enforcer. When the cops came for the enforcer, three cops went to the hospital with broken jaws and arms. Assault charges were added to the list of charges against the enforcer. The judge wasn't amused and gave the enforcer thirty years.

On his arrival at the prison, the enforcer, let it be known that he was top dog and if anybody did not like it they could always challenge him anywhere, anytime or any place. Word soon got back to Larry and Jeff that the enforcer was challenging them. Nobody knows what took place between Larry, Jeff, and the enforcer. The enforcer simply vanished. The prison was searched from top to bottom. After months of investigations, the state police gave up the search.

A few years later, one of the lead investigators was told that the enforcer was put into the prison heating furnace and incinerated. No one knew for sure who did it.

Larry and Jeff had a simple policy about anyone who failed to pay or would steal from them or challenge them: they would wind up in the prison infirmary with a broken arm or leg. One way or the other the miscreant would pay.

Once out of the joint, Larry and Jeff started to take over the drug sales in South Seattle. It wasn't too difficult to do. You had a bunch of low life pimps and drug suppliers who were small time hoods running the trade. Some of them had to be taught the order of things. As Larry's and Jeff's organization grew, they were able to enlist others to do the persuading. The bottom line was that they took over and ranthings.

Larry and Jeff became the suppliers. There was less risk associated with supplying rather than sales. If you got involved in sales, you ran the risk of coming to the attention of the police.

Larry and Jeff decided they would remain low level suppliers and avoid the larger traffickers who became targets of the DEA or the local Narcotics Units.

Both still maintained the rule that if you took something or failed to pay they hurt you. Today, they were going after "D" because he had failed to show to turn in his money from the week's sales.

"D" saw Larry as he was coming up the front porch. In a panic, he made a run through the house and kitchen to the back door. Just as he went through the dining room area and into the kitchen, he ran into Jeff who had been waiting. It did not take Larry and Jeff long to determine that "D" had squandered the money and drugs on a bunch of whores. Larry took great delight in breaking "D's" fingers then his arms. Finally the pair beat "D" into unconsciousness and threw him down the stairs into the feces and urine in the basement.

Just as Larry and Jeff were leaving, a squad car pulled up in front of the house. Officers were responding to a trespassing complaint from neighbors. Larry and Jeff were forced to go out the backdoor and escape. Lucky for "D" the officers had arrived. He was pulled from the basement and sent to the hospital.

Both Larry and Jeff had to go home and take a shower to rid themselves of the stench.

They were going to a party and had to get ready. If "D" survived, he would be required to come up with the money. That was the rule.

At the party, Larry was having a good time mingling. Jeff was a little more reticent. He was the paranoid one, always watching out for an attack. Both of them had made enemies and Jeff was always on the alert.

One time, his watchfulness paid off. Jeff was walking out of a restaurant with Larry when he noticed a person walking up to Larry. Jeff saw the guy was walking towards Larry and not taking his eyes off of him. Jeff got between the person, and Larry just in the nick of time. Jeff broke the guy's wrist and made him drop a knife he intended to use to kill Larry. It was late at night and there was no one around. Larry and Jeff loaded the clown into their SUV and took him for a ride.

It did not take Jeff long to get the information he needed from the knife wielder. It seemed that someone sold the attacker's sister a bad batch of coke which caused her to die. The attacker blamed the incident on Larry who had nothing to do with it. Just to make sure the attacker understood that it was not acceptable to assault Larry. Jeff broke his arm and dislocated his shoulder. Considering the circumstances, Jeff let him live.

Several weeks later the body of a drug dealer was found lying on the assailant's lawn. No suspect or motive was developed for the murder. The case was eventually closed for lack of any leads. Police did have a theory that the murder may have been retribution for the overdose of the assailant's sister. Once the police advanced that theory, Larry's assailant and the assailant's family quit cooperating with the police.

Some family members held the theory that this was a message that justice was served.

Larry was having a good time under the watchful eye of Jeff. Larry saw a black pimp by the name of "Uptown Brown" come into the room. What caught Larry's attention was the woman with him. She was barely twenty but gorgeous as far as Larry was concerned. It appeared Uptown had latched onto a good looker that would make him lots of money. Larry decided to check her out. When Uptown was off talking to someone or was in a side room snorting some coke, Larry made his move. Larry went up to the babe and struck up aconversation.

Larry soon learned that the girl was named Christy "CC" Copeland. She had met Uptown a couple of days before. Uptown had promised to show her how to make money and be a star. Uptown hadn't got to first base with "CC" yet but he figured tonight would be the night.

Christy was no fool. She had heard the pitch before. She had no intention of going to bed with this pimp or any other pimp. She had been working in Bars and Hotels as a call girl and strip dancer. She was starting to develop a clientele at dancing or hooking but her customers were not enough to make a good living. She was looking for other ways to increase her salary so to speak. Attending this party might lead to more contacts.

Christy as a child was lovely. She had a sunny disposition and a smile that would melt any heart. Her world consisted of dolls, Peter Pan and cartoons as any little girl would want as she grew up. Her parents were both professionals and made a good living for themselves and Christy. That was the problem.

Christy's parents ignored her. To her parents, toys and things were an expression of love.

They were never there for her. Unfortunately, things cannot compensate for time with your parents. Christy's parents felt that what little time they spent with her was quality time and that was all that was needed.

By the age of fourteen, Christy, began to steal. She did not need the items she took from stores. She did it to get attention. When she was caught, her parents tried to counsel her then continued to ignore her until the next time. Finally, she wound up in juvenile.

A judge gave her thirty days in juvenile ostensibly to teach her a lesson about breaking the law. She also got forty hours of community service and restitution which her parents paid. It was in juvenile that Christy changed. She came into contact with other juveniles who broke the law. She made friends with some of the smarter ones who had a plan of action to steal more when they got out. One girl who was a little older told Christy about making money as a prostitute. This girl was a street hooker, but Christy figured out it was safer to work bars and hotels than the streets where she would be victimized by pimps.

Christy thought about the prostitution angle a lot after she was released from juvie. Her parents were relieved to get her back and promptly started counseling for her. True to form, the parents would not attend the counseling sessions all the time. Christy just endured the humiliation until she could get out of the sessions. The counselor was an idiot and stared at Christy's legs and boobs. She found she could manipulate the guy with ease. She began to use her new found manipulative skills to control others. She began to realize that she had a commodity that others would pay a great deal for.

Christy developed a strategy. First, she would seduce a boy to see if she liked to have sex.

She found a willing patsy who relieved her of her virginity and gained the bragging rights for doing so.

She found a kid who had a connection that could make up fake Id's. At seventeen, Christy looked twenty five and was well endowed.

With a new perspective of what it would take to get ahead, Christy, who had taken the moniker "CC" turned a few tricks. She started to frequent night clubs looking for tricks. She became aware that strip dancing was more lucrative than hooking. It was not long before "CC" was a pole dancer in a strip joint. Because of her physical looks, "CC" was able to attract a large clientele. "CC" didn't like the low life scum clubs so she migrated to the more upscale clubs. Her tips from the scum that patronized these clubs were generous. She made a comfortable living.

Once in a while, she would turn a trick for a sugar daddy who was in town and loaded. More often than not she was able to separate her

John from his money and made him feel good while she was doing it. Many a John left her room flat broke but happy.

Her parents became irrelevant to her life style. When she was around them, she felt uncomfortable but was somewhat drawn to them. She would keep in contact with them albeit quite infrequently.

"CC" came close to entering the big time. She hooked a Hollywood producer who was in town on business. This guy liked "CC" so much that he decided to take her home and put her in one of his films. Her chance at stardom came to a screeching halt when the suspicious wife intervened. Besides the wife had photos taken by a private investigator hired to make sure she got lots of money in the divorce settlement if needed.

"CC" encountered Uptown Brown one night while she was dancing. Uptown had come into the club with a couple of cronies to just have a good time. From other dancers, "CC" learned that Uptown was a successful drug dealer. "CC" made a mental note to get to know this guy because he could lead her to a way to make more money. During her break, she made a point to talk to Uptown. Uptown took the bait and struck up a conversation with her.

Uptown was so enamored with "CC" that he came back the second night to see her. This time, Uptown invited "CC" to a private party at a local residence. "CC" immediately accepted because it would put her in contact with other drug dealers who might benefit her. "CC" had decided she would not be a street hustler or sell direct to users. She was determined to set up a network of dealers who would work for her. She would become the supplier and not the pusher. It was at this party that "CC" encountered Larry and Jeff.

When Larry first made his move on "CC", she didn't think much of him. When he persisted, "CC" started to listen to him. It was an acquired trait she had learned as a prostitute. She had found that a lot of men wanted to talk. Sometimes, they would talk to her as if she was their mother. It was the ability to listen that probably contributed to her success as a call girl.

After baring their souls, the Johns were willing to be very generous towards her.

As she listened to Larry talk, she began to realize that this guy was no fool. In short, order she was friends with Larry and Jeff. When Larry introduced Jeff, "CC" laid back and watched.

She realized that the two of them were best friends, and she needed to accept that relationship if she was to get close to Larry. At this first meeting, "CC" began to ingratiate herself into the friendship between Larry and Jeff. Jeff for the most part accepted the newcomer. Besides he liked women period and didn't like settling on one single broad. He figured that if the relationship between Larry and "CC" made Larry happy that was his business.

Uptown Brown, on the other hand, was not so impressed. When he came back into the main room, he found "CC" handing a business card to Larry. This was a blatant insult and a challenge, Uptown was not going to let this slide.

Uptown walked up to Larry, Jeff and "CC" and stated to Larry, "What the fuck are you doing with my woman, man?"

Larry looked up at Uptown and grinned. He replied, "We are just having a conversation." Uptown looked at Larry and said, "Get your punk ass outta here before I kick the shit outta you!"

Jeff recognized the danger immediately. He took one look at Larry and knew Larry was getting ready to kill this idiot. Jeff did not need a killing in a room full of witnesses. He got up and got close to Uptown's ear. He whispered, "Listen asshole this is not the time and place to settle this. Let's meet at Frink Park in an hour and we can settle this mano y mano. Uptown was arrogant and stupid enough to take Jeff up on his challenge."

Frink Park was a little out of the way place in the Capitol Hill, Madrona section of Seattle. It was a place where dopers met to pass the time or create drug deals. It lost its popularity after a local pimp killed a prostitute and dumped her body in the park. The gentleman who ruined the park for the others was eventually found with a bullet in his head. Over time, the cops began to forget about Frink Park and it returned to its status as neutral ground.

Uptown decided he should take a couple of guys with him just in case. When he arrived at the park, Larry was there waiting. There was no other person in the area. Uptown figured this was going to be a piece of cake. He would smash this prick's face in and call it a night and leave. Jeff had other ideas.

Jeff had concealed himself in the bushes. When Uptown and his two cronies stepped out of his Cadillac, Jeff waited until Uptown was near Larry then he emerged from the bushes with a sawed off shotgun. Jeff quietly slipped up behind the two body guards. He hit the first body guard and dropped him like a rock. As the second body guard turned to see what happened, Jeff hit him with the butt of the shotgun. The second body guard dropped to the ground as well.

Jeff then pointed the shotgun at Uptown and stated, "Like I said motherfucker, it would be *mano y mano.*"

Uptown looked nervous for a couple of seconds. Jeff again looked at him and stated, "Don't worry you little fuck, I am not going to kill you, he is,"pointing to Larry.

By now, Larry was upon Uptown. Without saying a word, Larry hit Uptown square in the jaw. Uptown reeled back from the blow.

Larry glared at Uptown then said, "Nobody talks to me like you did at the house you piece of shit. Not only am I going to stomp the shit out of you for the insult I am going to take your girl as well. I want you to know who is doing this to you and why."

Uptown charged at Larry. Larry simply stepped aside and landed a punch behind Uptown's ear. Uptown dropped like a rock. Larry then began to break Uptown's bones one at a time. There was a sickening snap as a bone broke. Larry would taunt Uptown as each bone snapped. Finally, Larry began to punch Uptown in the face until he was unrecognizable. By then Uptown was unconscious.

Jeff in the meantime had worked the two body guards over but kept them conscious.

When he got done beating on them, Jeff reminded them of what would happen to them if they decided to snitch. Both mumbled between broken teeth that they would not tell. Jeff let them go.

Uptown spent a week in intensive care and a month in the hospital mending.

Investigating officers could not get the three to talk so they eventually closed the case. No sleep was lost over three assholes getting theirs.

"CC" began to be a regular in the lives of Larry and Jeff. Both soon discovered that "CC" was no ditzy blond. She had a good head full of sense and caught on to the business right away. Sometimes, "CC" had a good intuition about people. A couple of times, she saved both Larry and Jeff from being busted by the cops. She organized and set up investigations of people who were admitted into the group. She was able to ferret out the suspicious ones. It wasn't long before she became a trusted companion to Larry and Jeff.

Things went pretty well for Larry, Jeff and CC for a while. Business was good and the money was starting to roll in. Larry and Jeff actually wore suits instead of their blue jeans when they were on business. CC had the best dresses and jewelry in town. Life was good.

It didn't happen overnight. Their downfall took some time. Larry and CC began to use more of their product. Jeff started to join in. Cocaine was in an unlimited supply. It wasn't long before all three were hooked on their own cocaine. After that the slide became faster and faster.

Uptown Brown had held a grudge for a while. He wanted to get even for Larry sending him to the hospital and taking CC. When he began to notice the increased drug habit of Larry, Jeff and CC formulated a plan to get even. It was simple, Uptown found a guy who got into Larry's drug sellers circle. He then made friends with an intermediary who he knew was a police snitch, and would sell his soul to the highest bidder. He also knew this snitch needed to work off a recent cocaine arrest. Uptown used him to give information to the local narcotics agents he had learned from his plant inside Larry and Jeff's circle of pushers. CC, who was normally cautious and hard to fool had become lax just like Larry and Jeff. She missed Uptown's plant.

Uptown was careful to not allow any of the snitch's info to be traced back to him. He new what would happen to him if Jeff or Larry found out the source of the information leak. It was really simple, the plant would tell Uptown what the three were up to. In turn, Uptown would find a way to tell the police snitch about Larry, Jeff and CC. It was usually in a casual conversation where Uptown would tell the snitch about Larry, Jeff, and CC's operation. To the snitch, Uptown was just nursing a grudge and complaining about Larry. The snitch never felt the info was being fed to him deliberately.

With the intel gathered from the snitch, the Seattle Police Narcotics unit was able to put together enough information to get a search warrant. The warrant not only covered Larry and CC's house plus Jeff's house, it also covered a storage building where the narcotics was being stored.

Information filed after service of the search warrant on Larry Oliver and Jeff Moore's homes plus a storage shed located on the property of Larry Oliver showed one pound of cocaine found in the storage shed along with narcotic paraphernalia to cut cocaine. At the residences of Oliver and Moore, over 500 grams of cocaine was seized. Fingerprint evidence showed that Larry Oliver, Jeff Moore and Christy Copeland had all handled the illegal cocaine. A fourth set of prints were identified as belonging to a drug dealer living in California. That person was not arrested and charged since constructive possession could not be proven.

Larry and CC were having breakfast when the doorbell rang. CC went to answer the door when it was suddenly forced open and uniformed SWAT officers and undercover narcotics forced their way in.

Jeff Moore was asleep when he heard his front and back door cave in. He had enough time to sit up in bed and grab his pistol from under his pillow before his bed was surrounded by uniformed SWAT officer with automatic weapons. When ordered to put his gun down, Jeff decided to comply. There were no percentages in trying to take on cops armed with automatic weapons.

Larry, Jeff, and CC were brought before King County Superior Court Judge Walter Wiggens. Judge Wiggens was presiding judge over the Drug Court for King County. All three pled not guilty and were granted bail of $50,000 each. That amount was reduced after the attorney for the defendants was successful in arguing for a reduced bail.

The arrest effectively put an end to the careers of Larry, Jeff, and CC. No one would touch them. It was felt that once you had been arrested, you would turn snitch in order to get probation or a reduced sentence.

Jeff and Larry were beyond enraged. They were like a pack of rabid dogs seeking a prey.

Larry had CC go over who could have snitched. It was not long before CC began to suspect Uptown Brown's Plant. Larry and Jeff weren't about to wait for proof. Anyone remotely suspected of snitching them off was a dead man.

Jeff and Larry went to the plant's apartment and waited for him to come home. The plant whose real name was Gary had a girlfriend named Dee who came home with him. Jeff and Larry waited until the two had gotten inside the apartment and were getting ready to sit down with a beer. Dee was fortunate, she was taken into the bathroom in the master bedroom where Jeff slit her throat.

Gary, the plant, wasn't so lucky. Larry tied him to his bed in full view of his dead girlfriend. First, Larry cut off Gary's pants and shorts. He looked at Gary and said, "I want to know who you were talking to at the cops and if anyone else was involved in this with you." Gary was defiant and spit at Larry.

Larry took a pair of pliers and went to work on Gary's testicles. It was not long before he had ruptured both of the testicles. Gary in the meantime had changed from defiance to begging for Larry's mercy. It did no good. Larry was going to get the information from Gary if it took a long time. Next, Larry started to remove Gary's fingernails, one at a time. Gary had begun to scream so Larry put a wad of hand towels in his mouth. Larry told Gary that all he had to do to stop the pain was to shake his head that he was ready to talk.

Gary finally signaled that he would talk after the last fingernail was removed from his left hand. Gary simply bowed to the inevitable. He knew that once he told Larry what he wanted he was going to die. Gary told Larry about Uptown Brown and how he set up the snitch to tell the Seattle Police Narcotics about Larry and Jeff. After Gary finished telling Larry all that he knew, Larry simply shot him in the head killing him instantly. It would be days before his body and the body of his girlfriend were discovered.

Larry and Jeff now had two names of the people who snitched on them. Larry found the snitch immediately. He was home watching some rerun about a hit man. When he answered the knock at the door, Larry and Jeff forced their way into the dingy apartment. Larry and Jeff tied him down to his bed just like they had done to Gary a few hours before.

The snitch was not so brave. He started to talk immediately. It wasn't too difficult to figure out that Larry and Jeff knew details about Uptown Brown otherwise they would not be standing over him in his bedroom. The snitch hoped to keep his life if he told Larry and Jeff everything immediately. At least, he would not have to endure hours of torture.

The snitch quickly told how Uptown had told him things which he passed on to the Seattle Police Narcotics Unit. Larry had figured out that the pathetic piece of shit in front of him did not realize he had been used by Uptown Brown. Larry did not waste any time with this slimy piece of shit. He shot the snitch in the head. For good measure, Jeff shot him in the chest.

Next, Larry and Jeff turned their ire on Uptown Brown. He would not be easy to grab as the other two had. Larry and Jeff laid out a plan to snatch him when he was most vulnerable.

Uptown frequented a bar in Seattle called the Fire Light in Downtown Seattle. Larry and Jeff would have to catch him as he came out late at night. Lucky for Larry and Jeff, after killing Gary and the snitch, it was Friday night. Uptown would go to his favorite night club for the evening. If they were lucky, Uptown would hook up with a whore or someone he knew and go home to spend the night.

Right at closing, Uptown came out of the Fire Light with a whore on his arm. It was at this point that things began to unravel for Larry and Jeff. As Uptown walked to a nearby parked car, Larry and Jeff approached him from behind. Jeff put his pistol into Uptown's back. Larry grabbed the whore and told her to get lost. Instead of taking the whore and killing her with Uptown, Larry had made a fatal mistake. The whore when approached by the Seattle Police Homicide Detectives investigating the death of Uptown Brown told them the names of Larry and Jeff. Based on the information the detectives would be able to put together DNA evidence linking the deaths of Gary, the snitch and Uptown Brown.

Larry and Jeff did not waste any time with Uptown. In a twenty-four hour period, the two exacted their revenge on Uptown. When Uptown would beg for mercy, Larry and Jeff would just taunt him more then proceed to find some new and painful way to make Uptown cry out in anguish. If Uptown passed out, he was revived and the torture would start over. In the end, Uptown was reduced to a blubbering mass of blood. There was not an inch of his body that did not have a bruise or knife cut on it.

Larry and Jeff did not have the humanity to spare Uptown even when he lay unconscious and bleeding for the last time. They just let him bleed out slowly until there was no blood left in his body. Once he was dead, Larry and Jeff took Uptown Brown to Frink Park and dumped what was left of him in the park. His body was only identified through fingerprints and DNA. His face was a bloody piece of meat and unrecognizable.

Detective John Thomas, the Seattle Police Homicide in day shift, had started his day off by going and having coffee at a nearby restaurant from his office. He had just finished up an assault case and had testified in a homicide case. For a change, his day was empty. He could relax and go through old assault cases that had not been taken care of yet. Most of the cases would be domestic violence or cases with no chance of identifying the suspect. The domestic violence would go to the domestic violence unit to handle. If there was no chance of identifying a suspect, those cases would be inactivated. Most of the misdemeanor cases involved a known person. In those cases, they would be referred directly to the court unit for charging. Detective Thomas did not know that he would soon be given a case that would remain with him until the day he died.

Detective Thomas had become a dichotomy to the police force. His upbringing was no different than most police officers. He came from a middle class home. His father worked at Boeing in Seattle. His mother had worked as a county civil servant. Thomas had two siblings, a brother and a sister. The sister was married and had two children. His brother was older and had been in construction for years. He owned his own company.

Detective Thomas had married before he became a police officer which is usually fatal to police marriages. Usually the wife is not accustomed to the odd hours and the danger. More often than not, it is the wife who initiates the divorce. Within two years after joining the police force, John's wife filed for divorce. Lucky for John, there were no children.

Most police officers who are divorced reach out to the next available person who will pay attention to them. Such was the case with John. He married a waitress shortly after his divorce.

That marriage did not last. After two years, Detective Thomas found himself alone once again.

One of the problems with John's marriages was he wanted to be your typical cop. He would stay late and drink with his buddies or go on fishing and hunting trips with his fellow officers. Divorce was inevitable.

After his second divorce, John continued to drink and have fun with other officers. Then he got a job in the homicide unit. All of a sudden, his whole perspective on life changed. He became more reserved and withdrawn. He no longer patronized the cop bars and did not attend as many social events as he did at first. John had developed a reputation as a "cop's cop" That all changed when he met Judy about the same time he was assigned to homicide.

John was attending a Christmas party at his brother's home. Judy had come with a couple of girl friends who knew his brother's wife. Judy had married at a young age. Her husband was a high school friend who rushed into marriage then failed to live up to his commitments. There were no children involved in the marriage which made the parting much easier.

John was sitting alone at a small table in the living room. As often happens at social gatherings, people tend to drift from one area to another to talk. Judy and her girlfriends eventually came to the table and sat down on the chairs next to John. Judy and John struck up a conversation. John soon found out that Judy was divorced, had no children and attended church on Sundays. He developed an instant liking for her.

John's sister in law was not stupid. She saw a perfect opportunity to pair her brother in law with a possible wife. At the first opportunity, John's sister in law invited John and Judy over for dinner. It was obvious what she was doing to everybody concerned. It worked. John and Judy began to see each other socially. In fact, they became good friends.

John soon lost all interest in police officers and police activities. He began to go out with non - police friends and attend family outings with Judy. This did not stop his police work. John built a reputation as a no nonsense investigator who was good at what he did.

Detective John Thomas was sitting at his desk thinking about calling Judy to see if she wanted to go out for dinner when his shift commander Lieutenant Bob Bergman motioned him into his office.

John came in and sat down. Lt. Bergman began, "John, I called you in here for a couple of reasons. Your sergeant is off for the next two weeks so I want you to be the acting sergeant for your squad. You will start the day shift tomorrow as acting sergeant. You are next on the sergeant's list. I hope to keep you in the unit when you make it. I understand Captain Walker is retiring next month. I am next to be promoted to Captain. Your sergeant will take the lieutenant's slot here. You will take the sergeant's slot I hope. However, that is not the only reason I called you in. We have had three homicides in the last week I feel may be connected. I want you to take the lead in the investigation."

The other shoe just dropped thought Detective Thomas.

Lt. Bergman went on, "The first homicide was discovered last night. A narcotics snitch was tied to his bed and executed. By itself, there does not appear to be any connection to other homicides except for the circumstantial evidence. This morning, two homicides were discovered while you were in court. The two victims were found in an apartment. A woman was found in the bath tub with her throat slit. Her boyfriend was found tied in his bed. The male victim had been beaten, tortured, and executed. The fourth body was found later in the morning in Frink Park. That victim had been tortured, beaten, and executed also. The MO on two of the victims are the same. I had a fast track ballistics report done on the bullets found in the bodies of the victim's. I just got off the phone with the lab. They verbally confirm that the bullets match two separate guns both used to execute three of the victims. I am assigning you these cases for follow up."

Detective Thomas could see that there was more to the story. He nodded and waited for the additional information.

Lt. Bergman let Detective Thomas digest the information before he went on. Then he began again. "I got a call from Narcotics. They say the informant may have been killed by a couple of guys who he had recently given evidence against. Narcotics says the snitch had failed to come to a scheduled meeting. When detectives went to his apartment they found him shot while tied to his bed."

Lt. Bergman went on, "The two dealers who may have done this are named Larry Oliver and Jeff Moore. Oliver has a girl friend named Christy Copeland who may have been an accomplice. All three were recently charged in Narcotics Court based on evidence obtained through information supplied by the snitch. Right now, we have no evidence linking these three to the murders."

Detective Thomas asked the obvious question, "Do we have any DNA evidence?"

"Not yet", replied Lt. Bergman. "It will take a few days."

"I am assuming the woman was just in the wrong place at the wrong time? That appears to be the case".

"Has the Evidence Units finished processing the scenes?"

"Not yet, they are still at the scenes. They should be done in a couple of hours. I was at the scene of a couple of homicides. They are not pretty. It looks like the one guy named Gary and the pimp Uptown Brown were deliberately tortured. There was a lot of rage in those killings."

"Okay, I will wait for the photos," said Detective Thomas. "I am going to go up to the Medical Examiner's office and attend them and see if I can learn anything else."

As Detective Thomas got up to leave, Lt. Bergman added, "Narcotics told me Uptown Brown was seen at the Fire Light night club on Sixth Avenue about four nights ago. He left with some whore named Debbie which is an alias for a Deborah Lynn King. She has an address of 1520 Boylston Street on Capitol Hill. If she is not at home you might try the Fire Light. She hangs out there a lot.

Narcotics and Vice are both watching out for her as well."

"Thanks", replied Detective Thomas.

Detective Thomas went straight to the Medical Examiner's office. Autopsies were in progress when he got there. The person who got the task of performing autopsies on the four victims was Hai Wan (Slugger) Choi. Choi earned the nickname of slugger because he could hit a ball out of the ball park. In his spare time, he coached little league baseball. Any police team lucky enough to get Slugger on their team was sure to win any game.

When Detective Thomas entered the autopsy room, Slugger looked up and stated, "Welcome to the meat locker detective. We have a special on steaks today."

Thomas just grinned and approached the table where a female was lying.

Slugger looked at Detective Thomas and stated, "It has been a while since I have seen such rage. This one here, pointing at the female, was lucky. She had her throat slit. There was no sign of torture. It appears she was in the wrong place at the wrong time. This one here, pointing at a male lying on a table next to the female, got off lucky too. He was shot once in the head and once in the abdomen. There were no signs of torture on him either. I wouldn't have connected him to the other murders but I got a call from Lt. Bergman asking me to remove any bullets for immediate processing. I did a quick x-ray and recovered all the bullets. I sent them to the lab and notified Bergman. Lt. Bergman called back later to alert me to the fact that the bullets removed from the two males were from the same guns. Apparently, two guns were used to execute the victims."

Detective Thomas responded, "Looking at these wounds, it appears that this victim was tortured to get information. Look at his genitals and how they are mutilated then look at the type of wounds. I'd say this one was tortured until he talked. It looks like this guy held out for a while. He must have been one strong son of a bitch."

Slugger then chimed in. "It appears that all four were killed within a few hours on the same day. The woman and the guy with the mutilated nuts must have been killed fairly early in the day. My guess is probably around ten to noon four days ago. The next victim was probably shot a little after ten in the morning about four days ago. The final victim that was so viciously beaten was probably killed around two in the morning about three days ago."

Detective Thomas observed, "This one here shot in the head but not tortured was the police snitch. He was not about to suffer the fate of these others. He probably gave up any information he had immediately in order to save his life. It didn't work. Next the suspects went to the house where the guy with the mutilated genitals lived. They must have surprised the guy and his girlfriend. The girlfriend was taken into the bedroom and killed. Her boyfriend was tied to the bed and tortured until he gave up the last victim. After killing the man and woman the suspects then found the last victim and tortured him slowly and painfully. This last person seemed to be the one the suspects focused in on. He must have endured a lot of pain before he was killed."

Detective Thomas went on, "We have ball practice Friday night and a game on Saturday morning. Are you going to make it?"

Slugger looked at Thomas and replied, "I will be there. I will be late for practice but no problem with the game. I'll see you there. I will have a full report for you by tomorrow on these victims."

"Thanks," replied Thomas. As he left the autopsy room, he threw his face mask in the receptacle set aside for medical waste.

At the office, Detective Thomas began the preliminary work to start a case file on the homicides. He prepared a case for each of the victims. Then he called records to get any photos or rap sheets on the victims plus any information on Larry Oliver, Jeff Moore and Christy Copeland.

Thomas decided that the records would take a while, so he decided to pay a visit to Deborah King the prostitute. He took Dave Rincon his partner in homicide with him as was the custom. First, they tried the Fire Light bar. Debbie was not there. Next, the detectives went to 1520 Boylston Avenue apartment 201 to contact Debbie.

Debbie had just gotten out of the shower when the two detectives knocked on her door.

At first, she did not want to acknowledge the door but whoever was there was persistent.

She went to the door and said, "Who is it?"

"Seattle Police Homicide." Came the answer, "We want to talk to you."

Debbie thought for a moment, why would a couple of homicide detectives want to talk to her? She did not know anything about a killing. She decided to let the pair in just to find out what was going on. She opened the door and let the detectives in.

Detective Thomas expected a small squalid apartment. He was surprised to see a fairly neat orderly apartment. There was no pimp or any indication of anyone else living in the apartment. Debbie had the two sit down on a couch while she sat in an overstuffed recliner that matched the couch.

Detective Thomas came directly to the point. He stated, "We are investigating the death of a person known as Uptown Brown. We are told that you were seen at the Fire Light Bar about four days ago is that true?"

Debbie looked surprised for a moment but responded after a few seconds. "I was there. We started to leave around midnight. I am not sure of the exact time. As we started to get into Uptown's car, two guys named Larry and Jeff came up to us.

They are called the "Dynamic Duo" and have a reputation for being ruthless. Larry grabbed me by the arm and told me to get lost. I wasn't about to get involved in whatever the three had a disagreement over. I got the hell out of there. I figured that Uptown would call me when he was ready."

"Is there anything else you can recall?" asked Detective Thomas.

"Well, there was one thing I did notice. Across the street was a black SUV with a blonde woman driving. She appeared to be waiting for someone or possibly Larry and Jeff. Like I said, I was not about to get involved in the dispute so I left and went back into the bar".

"We are going to need you to come with us and give us a statement on what you have just told us. While you are at it, you will have to take care of a probation violation warrant. You failed to carry out some part of your prostitution conviction," stated Detective Thomas.

"I know it", stated Debbie, "I was to do some community service at an old folks home. I couldn't stand the place so I left."

Debbie was taken to homicide for a statement and booking. Once the statement on what she had seen and heard the night Uptown Brown disappeared was taken then reviewed, she was taken to the King County Jail and booked on the warrant.

When Detective Thomas returned to homicide, there was a message from records that his information was ready for pick up. He went up to records and picked up the packets on each of the victims and suspects. He then returned to homicide.

Detective Thomas sat down at his desk and thought about this case. It appeared that the motivation for the killings was pure revenge. This Uptown Brown had set Larry Oliver and Jeff Moore up. Brown had set the two up over an old score or to take over the narcotics trade belonging to Oliver and Moore. Brown must have used one victim to gain information which was then fed to the police snitch. Narcotics then went after Oliver and Moore based on the info gathered from the snitch. Once Oliver and Moore were taken down, they got even. Oliver and Moore probably did not know who set them up. Somehow they figured out that one victim was feeding information to Uptown Brown. That victim was the first person who was beaten and tortured. His girlfriend just happened to be there when Oliver and Moore struck. She was collateral damage. Next, Oliver and Moore went to the police snitch. The snitch was not tortured so he must have given up any information he had immediately. Finally, Oliver and Moore found Uptown Brown and exacted their revenge. Now the question was how to prove his theory.

In reviewing the case, Thomas figured there were a couple of ways to connect Oliver and Moore to the killings. A knife had been used to cut the throat of Wendy Tredham, the girlfriend of Gary Garfield the victim who was so brutally tortured. A knife had been used to cut Garfield and Brown. According to the evidence slip, a large pocket knife had been found at the scene in Frink Park. It may have been used by a suspect. The knife was bloody and had a partial print probably a thumb print on the blade. There was blood evidence on the knife as well. Hopefully, this knife would reveal some usable evidence to link Oliver and Moore.

Thomas figured he might as well try and put the arm on Christy Copeland who was known as CC. She appeared to be the weak link. She was possibly at the scene and the driver when Uptown Brown AKA Mitchell Ray Brown was abducted. The question was when to approach this CC. If she was questioned too early she could tip off Oliver and Moore that the police wanted to question them about the killings of Brown et al. Thomas decided it was prudent to wait until the DNA and fingerprint evidence came in on the knife. Maybe a short lull would make the suspects think they had gotten away with the killings.

It was two days until Thomas heard from the state lab. A rush order had been given to expedite the processing of the evidence in the case. Given the number of killings and the high profile nature of the case everything was accelerated.

News media was everywhere looking for things to air. Detective Thomas was tight lipped about the case. There were too many leaks and he did not want any evidence to get out to the public that would warn the suspects. When he was asked about the case, Thomas would just state they were waiting for the lab to return with evidence from the crime scenes. He wouldn't even admit that the killings were connected. When asked if they were connected, Thomas would just state they were looking for the lab to return with any evidence to establish a connection.

Larry and Jeff were getting pretty smug about the whole affair. None of the TV reports indicated that the police had any idea they were connected to the killings or that the killings themselves were connected. They began to relax.

When the report came in, it was a treasure trove of evidence. DNA evidence was everywhere linking Larry Oliver and Jeff Moore to the victims. DNA has become a godsend to law enforcement and prosecutors and a bane to defense attorneys and their clients. DNA can be found on hair follicles, sweat, blood, saliva, skin cells, and sperm. Many people have been released from prison because of DNA evidence. It establishes without a doubt the identity of the perpetrator in any case where DNA is found.

In this case, DNA belonging to both Larry and Jeff were found on the ropes used to tie the victims to their beds. DNA was found on the clothing of all the victims which was identified as belonging to Larry and Jeff. DNA found on Gary's girlfriend, Wendy Tredham belonged to Jeff Moore alone. All the other victims had DNA on their bodies that belonged to both suspects.

The pocket knife was the key linking all three suspects to the killings. Blood from all the victims were found all over the knife. A partial print belonging to Jeff Moore was found on the larger blade. He had closed the bloody knife and left the print in blood.

The knife itself had three blades, a large blade, a medium blade, and a small blade.

The smaller blade did have some blood that was probably transferred from the large blade when Jeff closed the knife. On the small blade were fingernail scrapings belonging to Christy Copeland. She had used the knife to clean under her fingernails. That DNA would be enough to get a needle stuck in her arm for taking part in the killings. Those that kill together die together mused Detective Thomas.

There were two guns used to kill two of the victims. Bullets found in the bodies of the victims were matched and confirmed Lt. Bergman's earlier statement to Detective Thomas.

Bullet wounds were found in the head and torso of the three victims.

Based on the evidence supplied by the State of Washington Crime Lab, Detective Thomas obtained warrants for the arrest of Larry Oliver, Jeff Moore, and Christy Copeland. The hunt was on.

Larry, Jeff, and Christy were in Seaside Oregon sniffing coke at a beach house rented for the occasion. They were oblivious to the brewing storm around them. Jeff had hooked up with a girlfriend and had brought her along to the beach house. As far as they were concerned, life was good.

At Larry's house in Seattle, a team of SWAT guys kicked in his front door and scared the hell out of a house sitter named Melanie. Melanie had no idea where Larry was. She had been asked by CC to watch the house for them while they were away. CC had deliberately not given any contact information to Melanie because she wanted to get away. After the SWAT team left, she packed up and left.

Jeff's house wasn't much better. There was a guy there with two chicks lying in bed when the SWAT team came through the door. All three did not know anything. The Sergeant of the SWAT team thought, "These people are alive and they reproduce and vote!" In disgust, he walked out of the house. Soon after the SWAT team left, the trio left as well.

Larry became aware that something was wrong when he got home. His front door had been kicked in. CC and Larry exchanged glances. Larry took out his pistol and pushed the door open. Both CC and Larry checked the house and found it empty. CC turned to Larry and stated,

"I will call Melanie and find out what happened". CC took out her cell phone and dialed Melanie's phone number.

Melanie answered almost immediately. She had seen who was calling from her caller ID.

"CC, the cops busted into your house looking for you and Larry. I overheard them talking. You have an arrest warrant out for you and Larry for killing someone named Uptown Brown."

"How long ago were they here?" asked CC. "They were there three days ago".

"Listen, Melanie, we are going to have to leave for a while, can you watch over our place while we are away?

"Sure, but I am not going to stay there. Those cops in their soldier uniforms scared me to death when they busted in. When are you going to leave?"

"We will be out of here by tonight for sure. I will drop off the key at your place later today. Thanks for the tip honey. I'll see you soon."

CC hung the phone up and turned to Larry. "The cops are after us. They have a warrant for our arrest and for Jeff. We need to get out of here!"

Larry was stunned. Everything he had worked for had come to a halt. If the cops were looking for him they would have evidence to keep him in jail. He could not get away if he let himself get captured. He would have to run. Larry sat down in a chair to think. He had a friend in California he could count on. The first thing he needed to do was to call his buddy named Mike in Fresno. Larry could not use the house phone. He had a couple of burn phones in a drawer. One of them could be used to make the call. Larry went to a closet drawer and pulled a cell phone from the bottom of the drawer. He dialed a number in California. Mike answered almost immediately.

"Mike, this is Larry in Seattle. How are ya' doin'?"

Mike was hesitant but replied, "Okay man. What's going on?"

"I have a little problem with the pigs and I need a place to hide out for a while so I can figure out what to do. Do you have a place me and two friends can live for a short while?"

Mike responded, "I have a place in northern California you can live for a while. I use it to go fishing or hunting when I need to get away. When are you coming?" Larry stated, "We are leaving tomorrow and should be in California in a day and a half. I have some business I have to take care of here in Seattle before I come. It is probably not a good idea to talk on the phone too long. I will call you when we get to the Oregon border. Thanks man." Larry hung the phone up.

Larry turned to CC, "Go pack your clothes and get ready to go. I will take you to Beacon Hill and drop you off at Dan Perry's house. You can spend the night there. I will come and get you tomorrow evening and we can start for California." CC nodded in agreement and headed for the bedroom to pack.

Larry took a quick check out the window to make sure that there was no cops staking his place out then he too went to pack.

While packing, Larry called Jeff to warn him of the danger. Jeff had already called his friend to find out why his door was broken. He too had been told the cops were looking for him for murder. When he tried to call Larry, he did not answer. Jeff was not sure whether Larry had been caught or not. He tried to call CC's phone but that did not work either.

Jeff looked to see if there were any stake outs near his home. He did not spot any so he decided to pack and wait for Larry to call. If Larry did not call soon he was going to get out of town. Jeff figured that if Larry did not call then the cops have him. It wasn't long before Larry called. At first, Jeff did not recognize the number on his caller ID and almost didn't take the call. However, he knew Jeff could be calling on a burner phone to keep his main phone from being tracked. Jeff answered with a terse. "yeah".

Immediately, Larry started talking. "Jeff, the cops were here looking for us. We are going to have to get out of here as soon as we can. I have some cash stashed here at the house. What do you have?"

Jeff was always the planner who thought ahead. He replied, "I have a couple of banking accounts I have hidden with cash in them.

I can access them from anywhere. I also have a car we can use that is not registered in my name."

"Okay, just be careful. The cops could be anywhere. Get out of your house as soon as you can. I will take CC and drop her off at Dan Perry's house on Beacon Hill. I will meet you at Jefferson Golf Course at 3:00 o'clock near the Veterans Hospital. I will be in a blue Toyota".

Larry hung the phone up and went to pack some clothes. He needed something to calm his nerves so he sniffed a couple lines of cocaine. CC wasn't much better so she imbibed as well.

For the rest of the time, Larry got packed and went to see a real estate agent he knew.

Larry had made sure his friend was well taken care of since he needed to sell his real estate property in a hurry. Arrangements were made to sell the properties. Larry had set up an elaborate system to hide his money and property under false names and dummy corporations. So far, Larry had maintained his mental stability but the cocaine in his system was beginning to take a toll on his ability to think rationally.

Jeff was worse than Larry. He had become paranoid, angry, and homicidal. To Jeff, the whole world was after him. He couldn't understand how the cops had found out about Uptown Brown. "It had to be that whore I let go when we found Uptown," he thought. He was going to find that bitch and kill her. Jeff was blind with rage. All pretense of being the reasonable one of the three was gone. His only thought was to find Debra King and kill her.

Jeff tried Debbie's apartment and found it empty. He then went to the Fire Light bar to see if he could find her. He learned that Debbie was in King County Jail and was beyond his reach. That infuriated him more. He could not exact his revenge.

By the time Jeff returned to his home, he was so full of cocaine that he was no longer thinking he was just reacting. He grabbed his bag containing his clothes and went to get his car. He still had enough sense to remember that he had to meet Larry on Beacon Hill near the Veterans Hospital at 3:00 PM.

CC was high but she was cognizant enough to know she was in trouble. Through a cocaine fog she began to reflect on her life at the present. For some reason she felt she had to see her parents. She knew in her heart of hearts that she might not see her mother and father for a long time or possibly never. Remorse began to set into her consciousness. CC began to realize that maybe she had been wrong in not listening to her parents. Time after time her parents had been there but she did not pay attention to them. It was like they existed in her life in the background but she had paid no attention. CC didn't pay any attention to caution. While Larry was out at the real estate office, she walked out of the house and got into her car and drove off.

When Larry got back CC was gone. Larry was tired from the cocaine use. He lay down on his bed and took a short nap. When CC got back they would meet on Beacon Hill.

CC got onto Interstate Five from the Capitol Hill area where she and Larry had a home.

She headed north on the freeway. At the Lake City Exit, she took the off ramp. Lake City Way took her through the Northeast part of Seattle. CC's parents still lived in the same home in the Sand Point area of Seattle just to the north of Lake City. This is an area where the more affluent of Seattle live. As CC neared her parent's home, she became more anxious. She had not communicated with her parents for a couple of years. She was not sure how she would be received. Above all, she did not know whether her parents knew about the warrant for her arrest for murder.

When CC arrived in front of the house, she paused to gather herself. She knew deep down inside that this may be the last time she would see her parents. Gathering her strength she rang the doorbell. Shortly, her father appeared in the doorway. He seemed to be taken aback to see his daughter there. He simply stated, "Christy".

"It's me", responded CC.

"Come in, come in," replied her father.

Mr. Copeland took Christy by the arm and led her inside.

Once inside, Mr. Copeland called out to his wife, "Mother come see. Christy is here."

Within a short period of time Christy's mother emerged into the living room. "Christy, my child, how are you?" stated her mother. "Come, sit down."

For a short moment the silence was awkward, then, CC spoke up. "I am going away for some time and may not see you again for a while."

At that point Christy's mother broke down and started crying, her father spoke up.

"Christy, we know the police are looking for you and that so called boyfriend of yours. A nice police detective named Thomas came by the house the other day. He said that if you turn yourself in and cooperate he will see what he can do to help you."

The tears welled up in Christy's eyes. "It's too late dad," stated Christy as her voice broke and tears ran down her cheeks. She whirled around and ran for the door. She heard her father call out as she ran out the door, "Christy, we love you!"

Christy got into her car and sped off. After a few blocks, she pulled over and began to cry uncontrollably. After a short time, she regained her composure and drove off.

Christy had a sense of foreboding. Subconsciously, she knew she would not see her parents again. She began to have some recriminations about Larry and her life. Christy felt that she should prepare for the worst. Her first thoughts were that she would have to ditch all her credit cards and use cash only. There was a small out of the way branch to her bank where she could withdraw money. She would not be recognized there. At the bank, Christy went in and emptied her account. She took most of the money and secured it in her waist band. Then, she spread the money out between her jeans pockets and coat pockets. Luckily, the bank had the money onhand and the bank manager was agreeable.

Once she left the bank, she got into her car and drove to a nearby car rental office. She abandoned her vehicle and rented a car under one of her many aliases. She would use this car to rendezvous with Larry on Beacon Hill. From the rental office, she took 85th and drove west until she came to the I-5 on ramp. She got onto I-5 and headed south. As she passed the ship canal she could see Capitol Hill on her left and Lake Union on her right. Both areas had become picturesque through the years and had become home to Christy. A sudden sadness overtook Christy. She wanted so desperately to remain in this beautiful city.

After she passed through downtown Seattle, Christy took the Columbian Way exit to reach Beacon Hill. Beacon Hill Avenue was a split street that ran North and South through the southern part of Seattle. In the middle of the street was a meridian that partitioned the street into two halves. People would park in this meridian while they went shopping or visiting the local watering hole. If you went west from Beacon Avenue you would drop off the west side and into the flat lands of Seattle. Running along this west side of the hill was Interstate 5 that ran all the way from the Canadian Border to Southern California. The last street before the freeway and to the west of Beacon Avenue was 15th Ave. If you took 15th Avenue you could go from Dearborn Street to the south end of South Seattle before it curved around into Othello St Just west of the Van Assalt Police precinct, a distance of about five miles.

As Christy approached the intersection of Beacon and Alaskan Way, she saw Larry's car parked in the meridian. She pulled up next to him and got out. Christy put her bags into the trunk of Larry's car and got in. Jeff was in the backseat.

Larry looked at Christy and stated, "Jeff and I have some unfinished business to take care of. We will drop you off at Dan Perry's place then come back a little later. It should be getting dark by then."

"Okay," replied Christy.

Larry took Christy to a small house in a quiet middle class neighborhood. The homes were old but neatly kept up. He dropped Christy off in front of the house and told her he would be back. Christy took her purse and went inside.

Larry and Jeff had to go and settle their business. They went to the home of George Howard located in Rainier Valley which was just to the east of Beacon Hill. George was given all of the info on Larry and Jeff's narcotics dealings. Once the arrangements were made, Larry and Jeff left to meet Christy and make plans to leave town. As they pulled away from George's house it had gotten dark.

CHAPTER II

The Stop

Officer Moreland Lee was a good cop. He did not tolerate criminal behavior from his fellow officers or the citizenry at large. Officer Lee did not abuse prisoners or call them filthy names. He was a church goer, had a wife and two children. Officer Lee loved his job and his family. With what he had seen, he needed that strong bond between himself and his family. Without that strong family connection, he would have gone nuts.

Officer Lee was turning onto 15th Ave. S when a dark SUV went by him at a high rate of speed. Lee turned onto 15th Ave. South and fell in behind it. The officer paced the vehicle for three blocks then decided to stop it. Before he could turn on his overhead blue lights, the vehicle took a left turn and started up a small grade. Officer Lee got behind the vehicle and turned on his blue lights just as the vehicle pulled over to the curb.

Normally, a one man car will leave his blue lights on to attract attention especially if it is dark. By leaving his blue lights on, it is the hope of the officer that someone will watch and call in if any trouble develops. In this case, Officer Lee turned his blue lights off and left his red and amber lights flashing. He did light up the vehicle in front of him with his spotlight. There were two occupants and neither was making any furtive movements. As Officer Lee got out of his vehicle, the driver of the vehicle in front of him got out of his vehicle and walked to the sidewalk. This action did cause Officer Lee to be alert. Even if something was wrong, the officer was already committed. He would have to be alert.

Officer Lee had committed a cardinal sin in police work. He did not leave his blue overhead lights on to attract attention, and he did not call the license plate of the car into radio nor did he give radio his location for the stop. He had been trying to get to the precinct so he could change and go home. His wife and he were going out to dinner that evening. This caused him to be less aware of any danger. He simply wanted to go home. His intent was to give the driver a warning and leave.

Larry had a different perspective. He viewed the officer approaching him as a danger.

Larry had assumed the officer had given his location and the license plate of his vehicle to dispatch. Some operator at police headquarters was running the plate for wants and warrants. Nothing would be found. However, a backup unit was surely on the way to assist this officer. Larry did not know that it was shift change and no unit was coming since Officer Lee had not called the stop in. Most of the units were headed to the barn to go home. Larry wasn't sure what to do. He had to pick up Christy and get the hell out of there.

Officer Lee began to develop a certain anxiety about the whole affair when Jeff exited the vehicle and stood by the vehicle listening to what was transpiring. The officer saw the female exit the house next to the stop. He did not pay much attention to her, but instead chose to concentrate on the two men who were close to him on the sidewalk. The female walked past him and the driver. Just as she did so she suddenly turned around and pointed a gun at the officer.

"Don't move!" ordered Christy.

Officer Lee's worst fears were realized. He had treated the stop as just routine. His failure to call the stop in or leave his overhead lights on had created a case where simple time tested procedures would have prevented this from happening. Now, he was faced with a deadly situation and no one knew where he was since he had not called the stop in. Added to the problem was the fact that both Larry and Jeff had pulled their weapons and had them trained on the officer.

Larry immediately took charge. "Kneel on the ground with your hands behind your head," ordered Larry. Officer Lee did not have any choice so he complied. Jeff took the officer's handcuffs and handcuffed him with his arms behind him. He had learned that trick in prison.

Next, Larry and Jeff picked the officer up and put him in the back of the car on the passenger side. Another trick they had learned in prison. This protected the driver in case the prisoner got loose.

Larry instructed Jeff and Christy to wait by the car while he went inside and talked with Dan Perry. As Larry got to the front door, Dan opened the door and stated, "Are you crazy? You just kidnapped a pig." Dan had seen the whole thing from his front window. Larry responded that he at least had a hostage if he got into a confrontation with any police officer. Larry told Dan he was going to West Seattle to Jack Wakefield's house then he would head out for California.

Larry picked up Christy's purse and left.

Chapter III

The Phone Call

It was a slow night at the 911 dispatch center. There were the usual accidents, noise complaints, and domestic violence calls. Overall it was boring. Jenny McGowan had just returned from her break and was settling down to reading a romance novel she had found on a table in the break room. There was an almost inaudible buzz in her ear indicating a caller was being routed to her. Her first instinct was to look at the Ani – Ali display to see who was calling. It showed no information on the caller. Jenny stated, "Operator 67 what is your emergency?" An elderly voice on the line stated, "They have taken the officer. His car is parked in the 4600 hundred block of 17th Avenue South." For a second, Jenny was stunned at the information, then her training kicked in. "Who took the officer?" Jenny asked. The caller remained silent. "What is your name?" asked Jenny. The caller responded, "I can't tell you, but you must hurry." "What is your address?" asked Jenny. At that point, the caller hungup.

Jenny punched a button that went straight to the Chief Dispatcher. There were a couple of rings and the Chief Dispatcher came on the line.

The familiar voice of Daryl Smallworth came on the line, "Chief Dispatcher." Jenny stated, "We just had a hang up call. What sounded like an older woman stated that an officer had been taken and his car was still parked in the 4600 block of 17th Avenue South. There is no Ani – Ali information call on who called it in or their address. All we have is a person stating that an officer had been taken and his vehicle is parked in the 4600 block of 17th Avenue South. Looks like the phone call may have come from a prepaid cell phone."

As with all emergency calls requiring that all units be notified of a major incident, a tone is sent out with the information following.

Chief Dispatcher Smallworth hit the tone button on his console then broadcast, "Information for units in the South End, we just received a hang up call indicating a police officer has been taken in the 4600 block of 17th Avenue South. The caller indicated the officer's car is still parked at that location. Do we have any unit at that location?"

There was no response to the inquiry. Smallworth then keyed his mike and asked if there was a unit available to check the location. Two Robert Two and Two Robert Four, both late cars responded they would check. The two Sam District Cars who were responsible for the area were both in the station with an arrest.

Chapter IV

The Discovery

Two Robert Two was the first unit to reach the area. The two officers in the car could see the small overhead lights flashing. They approached the area cautiously since there was an anonymous complainant. No one appeared to be near the police vehicle. Two Robert Two took their time approaching the vehicle. There were past incidents where officers were ambushed after responding to bogus calls. The officers had their lights off on approach. One officer got out of the patrol car near the corner while the other officer drove up to the empty police cruiser. When they were satisfied that there was no one around the officer called into dispatch.

"Two Robert Two to radio."

"Two Robert Two," came the reply.

"We have arrived. The police unit is here but there is no one around."

"Received Two Robert Two, I will notify Three Robert and the watch commander."

About that time, Two Robert Four arrived and put his spotlight on the empty vehicle.

Officer Metz of Two Robert Four got out of his vehicle and walked up to Officer Hilton of Two Robert Two and remarked, "He is probably inside one of these houses with some chippie. He is going to be real embarrassed when we find him."

Officer Hilton responded, "I am not so sure. Look at the angle of the vehicle. It looks like it was angled as if there was a traffic stop. The car is not legally parked at the curb."

About then, Officer Guich came up to the pair. He had heard part of the conversation between the two. "I heard what you said about the chippie. Officer Moreland Lee is driving this car. His log sheet shows he is Two Robert One. He had been on a burglary report in Sam sector earlier. Must have completed the report and was headed in for the night. He is a straight arrow and would not have a chippie."

That was enough for Officer Hilton. He keyed his mike and stated, "Two Robert Two." The dispatcher replied immediately, "Two Robert Two."

"Two Robert Two we need to set up a quadrant search and has a supervisor been notified?"

"That is affirmative Two Robert Two. Three Robert and Car 233 are responding from the station."

At that point, Three Robert, a Sergeant Miles came on the air and stated, "This is Three Robert. My ETA is about two minutes." Car 233, a Lieutenant Cain, came on the air and announced he was right behind Sergeant Miles.

Within a couple of minutes both supervisors had arrived on the scene. Sergeant Miles took charge of the tactical situation. Lieutenant Cain basically stood around and listened.

The first order of business was to organize a search of the immediate area. When that was done, Sergeant Miles started to organize a door to door search. By this point, there were police cars all over the place. Traffic units were involved, off duty officers, even a couple of cars from the adjoining precinct had arrived. Plain clothes officers from headquarters and a couple of detective units had joined the search. Most had heard the request for a supervisor and a quadrant search. This meant that a serious problem involving a police officer was ongoing. It also meant that no effort would be spared to locate and help that officer. Lord, help the perpetrator if they were caught.

Three Sam Two, Officer Sara Styles, arrived at the scene and was immediately assigned to go door to door to locate any witnesses.

Chapter V

Alice

Sara took stock of the row of homes in front of her. Most people were either looking out the window or on the porch watching the large police presence that had suddenly appeared in their neighborhood. Some were talking to officers canvassing the neighborhood. Sara was attracted to a small neatly kept up home. This home did not have any lights on and no one seemed to be at home. As Sara fixed her gaze on the house, she noticed a slight movement of the front window curtain. Sara asked a nearby officer if anyone had talked to the occupant inside the home. The officer replied that his partner had knocked on the door but got no response so he left.

Sara decided to recheck the home again. As she approached the front entrance, she saw the face of an old woman appear behind the front window curtain. Just as suddenly as the face appeared, it disappeared. Sara knocked on the front door. She got no response.

She knocked again. She heard a faint, "Go away!" Sara wasn't sure what to do. Sara got up close to the door and said, "Ma'am, I know you are afraid but if you saw anything I need to know. A police officer has disappeared and we are trying to find out what happened." The reply was soon in coming, "I've told you all I can now leave me alone." Sara realized she was talking to the person who had called 911.

Sara responded, "Ma'am, I know the missing officer. He is a good man. He has a wife and two beautiful children. He should not be left to die or be killed outright by some scum. My name is Sara what is your name?"

The Rescue of the Officer Moreland Lee

The voice on the other side of the door was instantaneous, "Go away and leave me alone!"

Sara tried one more time, "Ma'am, will you please talk to me? An officer's life may depend on what you tell me".

There was silence. Sara decided to go tell the sergeant what she had found. There was no other recourse. There was no way to force this woman to talk.

As Sara turned to walk away the front door cracked open about two inches. A voice inside said, "Come in quickly!"

Sara was in such a hurry to get inside that she almost tripped on the door jamb. Once inside, she saw a frail really old woman standing there. The old woman was shaking and trembling.

Sara her to a small divan and sat her down.

"Like I said, I am Sara. What is your name?"

"My name is Alice," responded the old woman. "I live here."

"Did you see what happened to the police officer?"

"Yes. The officer pulled up behind this car that had just parked. At first, the officer had his blue lights flashing but he turned them off. Just as he did, the driver got out of the car and walked up onto the sidewalk. At the same time, the officer got out of his police car and walked to the sidewalk. As the driver and police officer got to the sidewalk, a woman came out of the light blue house three doors down and across the street. She walked toward the officer and the driver. About then, the car passenger got out and stood by the rear of the vehicle. By then the woman was just passing the driver and the officer. As the woman passed the two, she suddenly turned to the officer and said something to him. I could not hear what was being said. The driver and passenger both seemed to pull something out of their clothing and pointed at the officer. The objects looked like guns of some sort. The driver said something to the officer which caused him to kneel down. The passenger took the officer's handcuffs and put them on the officer. The officer was taken by the two and put in the back seat of the driver's car. The driver went inside the light blue house briefly. When he came out he had a purse or some kind of bag.

They got into the car and drove off. I called 911 while the driver was in the house but you did not get here in time. "You won't make me go out where I will be seen will you?"

"No ma'am, we won't. You stay inside the house."

Sara eased out the front door and onto the porch. She looked around to see if anyone had paid attention to her as she exited. Satisfied that no one was watching, she walked as fast as she could to Sergeant Miles and Lieutenant Cain.

Sergeant Miles looked up and saw Sara hurriedly approaching. Sergeant Miles secretly adored Sara. She reminded him of his daughter who had disappeared years before. She had been taken by a vindictive ex - wife who left a note saying she was taking their daughter and leaving him. Miles had tried to find his daughter but he had no money. He soon gave up hope. About two years after the Moreland Lee incident, Sara was diagnosed with bone cancer. A desperate ex – wife contacted Miles and begged him to be tested to see if he was a donor match. The ex had to admit that Sara was Sgt. Miles' daughter. The test showed that he was in fact Sara's Father. He was able to save his daughter.

As Sara approached, Sgt. Miles looked at her. He could tell something was wrong. "What's up?" he asked. Sara told the sergeant what Alice had told him. She pointed the house in question out to the sergeant and lieutenant. She could see the Sgt.'s face turn beet red. She swore she saw lightning bolts coming out of his eyes. There was one thing for sure, this man was pissed!

Sergeant Miles called to radio and asked for some units to meet him at the scene. That signaled that something was afoot. Within minutes, the street was flooded with grim faced police officers. The entire suspect house was surrounded by a sea of blue.

Chapter VI

Sergeant Miles

Sergeant Miles was considered a throwback to an earlier time. He was over six foot and barrel chested. His stomach had lapped over his belt years ago. He used to suck on a cigar years before but he succumbed to peer pressure a long time ago. Secretly when no one was looking he would imbibe. He was an old confirmed bachelor though occasionally one could spot an occasional blond leave his house with a smile on her face. On the surface, he appeared to be old and out of shape. Many a suspect had found out the hard way that this old man was strong as an ox. If he hit you, you went down and didn't get up for a while. Sergeant miles had been the golden gloves heavy weight champion for years.

One day, the sergeant was walking through the gym located in the police station. A young arrogant officer whose father was an assistant chief saw him and decided to teach this old man a lesson. Now sergeant Miles had had a bad day. A young street punk had called him some filthy names. The sergeant couldn't retaliate because there were too many people around. Some liberal twit would probably object if he laid a hand on this poor misguided black person who had to suffer under a white biased society. It didn't matter that this poor misguided person was in the process of beating the hell out of his whore for not making him enough money. When the pretty boy challenged the sergeant to a boxing match, Miles lost it.

Miles looked at this young jack ass and stated, "Okay, I have a few seconds." That statement implied that the young officer in front of him would only take a few seconds to dispatch. The officer's name was Howe. He knew he was going to be promoted and would have an easy path to leadership in the police department. Officer Howe looked at the old sergeant and said, "Do you need help putting the gloves on old man? Don't want you to hurt yourself." Miles said nothing. Some of the other younger officers had gathered around Howe and were encouraging him.

Both of the combatants stepped onto the mat and began. Officer Howe threw a couple of jabs and moved in for the kill. He woke up in the hospital with his jaw wired shut. A nurse told him it would be a couple of weeks before he would be able to eat anything other than soup.

Chief Howe took a dim view of the incident. There was nothing wrong with what the sergeant did. He was engaged in a legally sanctioned sport. However, the sergeant had humiliated his son and him. He was not going to allow that to go by. Chief Howe had Sergeant Miles transferred to the South Precinct. He was going to see that the sergeant stayed there until his retirement.

Sergeant Miles, true to form walked up to the front door of the home and knocked loudly on the door. When the door cracked open, he simply forced it open the rest of the way.

Officers poured inside.

Dan Perry was no slouch when it came to fighting. He had become top dog in boxing tournaments held in prison. A grudging respect developed between Larry and Jeff in prison. Larry and Jeff were dangerous. They would kill you when you weren't looking. Dan would just knock you flat. Larry often wondered if he could take Dan, but decided it was better to be his friend.

Dan had watched with amusement as the officers milled around outside his house. His amusement turned to concern when all of a sudden the cops focused in on his house. The next thing he knew the old sergeant who had been around the valley for years forced his way into his house along with half of the cops in the city.

The first person to react to the police coming through the door was Dan's girlfriend, Jennie. She had a big mouth that got Dan in lots of fights especially when she was a little lit. Jennie jumped up out of a chair she was sitting in and yelled, "You motherfucking pigs you can't bust in here li…". That was as far as she got when a police officer backhanded her knocking her back into the chair. The punch was so hard that the chair tipped over. It took Jennie a couple of minutes to regain her senses. She decided it was better to keep her mouth shut. These cops looked mean and serious.

Dan was more aggressive. He was an excellent fighter and had not lost a fight for a long time. When Sergeant Miles pushed his way into the living room, Dan immediately recognized him from past incidents. He wasn't about to be pushed around by this fat pig. Besides he had wanted a chance at this pig for a long time. His time had come. Dan's reaction was to plant a round house squarely on the jaw of the sergeant. Dan remembered swinging but did not quite comprehend how he got partly on the floor and partly on the couch clear across the room from where he was standing. Dan got to his feet just as the sergeant reached him. He once again tried to hit the sergeant only to find himself waking up on the couch. Once again the sergeant was coming toward him. This time Dan was not able to get up as quickly. The sergeant reached down, picked Dan up and flung him across the room and into a wall. As Dan's knees buckled, a painting hanging on the wall came loose and came crashing down onto his head. The sergeant was there again. This time he picked Dan up by the throat and slammed him into the wall.

For the first time the sergeant spoke, "Asshole, a woman and a man who kidnapped a police officer came out of this house, got into a car and left with the policeman. We want to know who they are and where they went!" Dan tried to speak but couldn't because the sergeant had him by the throat and he couldn't breathe.

Lieutenant Cain had been watching as Sergeant Miles had knocked the occupant of the house across the living room and onto a couch. Lucky for the occupant there was a couch or he could have been seriously injured. Before the Lieutenant could react, the occupant had arisen from the couch a second time. Sergeant Miles was on him again and threw him against the wall across the living room. Sergeant Miles then picked the hapless man up and was holding him by the throat against the wall.

Lieutenant Cain had spent most of his career in administrative jobs. His street time was limited. Once he made sergeant, he was sent to internal investigations. When he made lieutenant, he was transferred to patrol to get some patrol experience so he could be assigned to some other administrative unit and promoted to captain. He was aghast at Sergeant Miles' conduct. He started to step in and stop this travesty. As he moved forward to intervene, two officers stepped in front of him effectively blocking his way. The lieutenant could see in their eyes that had he tried to interfere these two officers would probably knock the crap out of him. At that point the lieutenant decided discretion was the better part of valor and backed off. He had just received his first street lesson that basically said if you kidnap or kill an officer all street etiquette was off. The police were going to get you no matter what it took.

Dan was in total shock. He could not breathe nor could he fight back. This old pig had him by the throat and he was losing consciousness. Never had Dan experienced such a total defeat. His only thought was to get his breath back. He was afraid for the first time in his life. He was so afraid that he started to pee his pants. Just as he started to black out from lack of oxygen, the old pig slackened his grip enough so that Dan could Catch his breath. Once again, the old pig asked Dan who had taken the officer. Dan was so afraid by then that he would have ratted his own mother out to get his air back.

Dan was barely able to squeak out, "It was Larry, Jeff, and "CC" who took him. They are going to West Seattle to Jack Wakefield's house." Sergeant Miles let Dan go. He promptly slid to the floor gasping for air.

Lieutenant Cain had taken this all in. He realized that now was not the time to raise the issue but he would charge Sergeant Miles with numerous violations as soon as this event was over. Lieutenant Cain would get his way eventually. The Chief of Police would prevail on the prosecutor to let him handle the incident in house considering the circumstances. The Chief gave Sergeant Miles two weeks suspension. The Seattle Police Guild, a union that represented officers, negotiated the suspension to the loss of holidays. Officers from all over the department gave up some holidays to make up for Sgt. Miles' loss. As for Lieutenant Cain, he became a pariah for his actions. He eventually moved to another department and became chief there.

Chapter VII

The Raid

Jack Wakefield was not having a good evening. He had gotten into a fight over some dope being stolen. Then his old lady, Toni, had mouthed off to some dude in a local watering hole. It was a tough fight but Jack had won. No sooner had he got home when Larry, Jeff and CC had pulled up at the front of his house. Jack knew through the grapevine that Larry and Jeff were wanted. He had three pounds of weed and a couple keys of coke stored in his basement. The last thing he needed was for the cops to come looking around his house.

As the three got out of their car, Jack walked up to the three and greeted them in a civil manner. He wanted to get rid of these three as soon as he could but did not want to make Larry or Jeff angry. Jack knew how dangerous these two were. Jack was surprised when Larry told him he wanted to turn his operation in West Seattle over to him.

Jack stammered a little and said, "I don't know what to say. I hear you and Jeff have had some bad luck with the police. Are you going to stick around or are you leaving town?"

Larry replied, "The snitches that caused all the problems are taken care of. No worry there. I will give you the names of all my contacts and you can carry on with business as usual. How about a price of fifty thousand?"

That was a steal as far as Jack was concerned. Jack replied, "Come on inside. I have that amount stashed away for emergencies."

Larry, Jeff and Jack went inside along with Jack's girlfriend, Toni. Jolene, Toni's girlfriend, decided to stay outside and talk to "CC" while Jack was inside with Larry and Jeff. While Jolene was talking to "CC" she saw the officer lying on the floor in the rear. Jolene said nothing. She did not want to start a fight with a cop handcuffed in the back of Larry's car.

In a few minutes, Larry, Jeff, and Jack came out of the house. Larry and Jack shook hands. Larry, Jeff, and "CC" got into their car and left. Jack breathed a sigh of relief. After the shock wore off Jack decided it was time for a celebration. Jack, Toni and Jolene went inside to celebrate.

In a short period of time, Jack had doubled his organization and became the undisputed dealer in all of Southwest Seattle. He had done this for a mere fifty grand.

Jack was feeling magnanimous so he decided to share his good fortune with Jolene and Toni. Jack had Jolene go to the basement to retrieve some coke and marijuana from his stash on a shelf in the back. Jolene was beginning to feel high from the small amount of coke she had shared with Jack and Toni just before she went to the basement to retrieve more. Jolene reached the bottom of the stairs and was just about to turn to get the dope when a noise caused her to turn and look around. She saw a helmeted face dressed in black about to enter the basement through a window. Jolene was taken aback by this figure. She started to scream and turned to run up the stairs. As she did so she stumbled and fell over a box. Jolene sat up to get her bearings. She saw one black clad figure already in the room and another coming through. The figure nearest to her had what looked like an automatic weapon pointed at her. By then the basement was filling up with black clad men. Jolene was not about to argue with these people. They looked grim faced and serious.

One of the men whispered to her quietly, "Turn on your stomach and put your hands behind your head." Jolene knew better than to argue. This man was serious and besides he had a big gun. She rolled over and put her hands behind her head. She felt a sense of relief when one of the men put handcuffs on her wrists. She knew these were cops who would not shoot her without cause.

Upstairs, Jack and Toni were lounging on the living room couch waiting for Jolene to return with the dope to continue to get high. Both the front door and the kitchen door splintered at the same time.

Men dressed in black, carrying automatic weapons burst in. One group went down the hall to check the bedrooms. Another group came into the living room and pointed their guns at Jack and Toni.

Jack reacted by jumping behind the couch.

Toni fell to the floor screaming, "Oh god! Don't kill me!" She then started to cry.

A rather large person came up to Jack and literally pulled him from back of the couch.

This person growled, "Come here, you piece of shit." He then slapped Jack so hard that Jack went flying across the room and wound up in stuffed chair. Another man picked Jack up and backhanded him, sending him flying back across the room. Another man picked Jack up by the throat and said, "Where is the officer, asshole?" By this time, Jack was disoriented and semi- conscious. He only tried to stammer. Nothing came out of his mouth but a lot of saliva and jibberish.

By then, Jolene had been brought up from the basement. All three miscreant were thrown on a couch. One person came up to Jack and shoved a gun in his mouth. "Where is the officer asshole?" said the man. Jack had a gun in his mouth and could not respond. He reacted by peeing his pants. Jack was sure he was going to die.

Between sobs, Jolene, saved the day, she cried out, "Don't kill him! I know what happened!" Jolene started whimpering, "I saw him! I saw him! He was alive. "CC" was guarding him while Larry and Jack were inside. When Jack came outside Larry, "CC" and Jeff got into the car and left.

"Please don't hurt us. Jack and Toni didn't know about the cop."

When the gun was removed from Jack's mouth, he knew he was safe. His arrogance started to come out of his mouth. Jack was able to wipe the trickle of blood from the corner of his mouth just as the nearest cop again backhanded him, knocking him over the coffee table and onto the couch.

"Listen, asshole! Keep your mouth shut and do what you are told!" said the big cop that had put the gun in Jack's mouth. "You are going to tell us the license plate and description of the vehicle these scum left in or I will kill you."

At that point, Jack, felt it was in his best interest to tell these pigs what they wanted to know and get them out of his life.

Shortly, a description of the suspect vehicle and license was broadcast state wide.

Homicide detective, John Thomas, was at his desk when the news of the raid reached him. He wondered if the suspects would be found in time to save the officer.

Chapter VIII

Maria

Maria Elena Estrada Lee was a quiet and solid woman who got things done. She was active in the community and earned a reputation as a "can do" person who had a willing ear and a helping hand when needed. She had been married to Officer Moreland Lee for fourteen years. She loved him today as much as she did when she first met him.

Their first meeting was inauspicious. She was coming out of a grocery store with her mother. The grocery bag handle broke and its contents spilled onto the ground. A young Gringo stopped to help pick up the spilled grocery items. Maria was kinda attracted to this Gringo and thanked him when the groceries were finally secure in her car. Later she saw him from a distance at a local gas station. She seemed oddly attracted to this Gringo.

Maria was of Mexican descent but was not a rabid activist for immigration rights. Her parents were illegal immigrants who had taken advantage of amnesty under Ronald Regan. They had paid their fines and got a green card. Eventually, they became citizens of the United States.

Maria herself was born in the United States in Bakersfield California at the Kern Memorial Community Hospital, affectionately known as "KMC". At an early age, Maria and her family moved to a suburb of Seattle known as Bothell. There she attended school in the elementary, junior high and high school schools. She had excelled in all grades and was recognized for her abilities. Her father got a job as a junior high school janitor. They didn't have a lot of money but they got by.

Once out of high school, Maria, got a part-time job at a local mall while she attended community college. Just before she was to graduate from college, she had her second encounter with officer lee. The next time she was to encounter Officer Lee she was on the side of the road with a flat tire. She was quite surprised when the officer pulled up in his private vehicle and stepped out in his uniform covered by a thin jacket. She instantly recognized him from the grocery store and the gas station.

Officer Lee approached the hapless Maria and stated, "Need help?" Maria was stunned.

She started to say something but could only stammer. Once she recovered from the shock of seeing this Gringo again, she started to speak.

"I could sure use a hand. I don't know where the jack is or how to put it together."

Moreland could see that Maria needed help so he took charge. He went to the trunk and found the jack and jack stand. Before long he had the spare tire on the car and the jack securely back in the trunk. When he was done he closed the lid to the trunk. He looked at Maria and said,

"That will do it".

"Thank you," replied Maria.

"What is your name?" asked Moreland.

"Maria Estrada," came the answer.

"I am Moreland Lee."

Moreland Lee did not volunteer that he had seen Maria around town and had wanted to meet her. The opportunity had presented itself and Moreland decided to jump on it. He had been curious about her ever since he had seen her at the neighborhood grocery with her mother. Her groceries had spilled on the ground so he helped pick them up. Since then he had been curious as to who she was. Moreland had taken her license number and the first chance he had, he ran it through the police computer. It had come back to her at a Bothell Address. Since then Moreland had been trying to figure out a way of meeting her. He had seen Maria at a gas station but did not approach her. When he found her stranded on the side of the road he jumped at the opportunity to meet her. Now he was thinking of a way to get to know her better.

Maria was glad when Moreland stopped to assist. When she saw the uniform under the jacket, she just knew her knight in shining armor was going to be arrogant and officious. His gentle smile and willing hand soon dispelled any doubts she had about him. Now she too was trying to find a way to get to know him without seeming forward.

For a few seconds, the two just kinda stared at each other and the ground. Moreland was the first to break the ice. "There is a small restaurant just up the road. Would you like to stop in and have a latte before you have to go home?"

Maria immediately accepted the invitation.

It took about a month for Maria's parents to come to the realization that their daughter had fallen in love with a Gringo and a cop on top of it all. The family had finally been accepted into American society.

It wasn't long before Moreland and Maria had established a living for themselves. They bought a house with a big picture window and six bedrooms. Moreland took over one bedroom for a den. Maria took another for her crafts and sewing room. The arrangement worked out fine. It wasn't long before the children started to come. There were two children to keep Maria busy while Moreland worked.

Maria elected to stay home and take care of the children instead of seeking a job outside the home. To keep busy, she became active in her church administering to the sick and needy.

She volunteered to help at the kids' school and got herself elected as president of the PTA. Of course, that soon led to her being elected to the school board. To top it all off, she was the editor of her local church newsletter. At Christmas time, she even found time to bake cookies to give throughout the neighborhood.

Maria had heard stories about police officers being shot. She knew there were some risks associated with her husband's job. She accepted the risk and put it in the back of her mind.

When she saw the dark police car with antennas sticking out all over she stopped what she was doing and watched as two people in uniforms got out of the car and approached her door. One officer had a star on his shoulder. The other wore crosses on his shoulders indicating he was a Chaplin. Something deep inside her told Maria that something was wrong. She wondered why these two men were coming to her home. She thought that Moreland was due home soon and he would have to speak to these two. A sense of dread suddenly filled her being. Then the doorbell rang.

As Maria opened the door she looked up the cul-de-sac where she lived. She saw two local police cruiser pull into the cul-de-sac. The man in the chaplain's uniform spoke first.

"Are you Mrs. Moreland Lee?"

"I am," replied Maria.

"Can I help you?"

"May we come in," asked the Chaplin.

Maria opened the door wider and stepped back to allow the men to come in.

"Mrs. Lee, I am Assistant Chief Brooks, and this is Chaplin George of the Seattle Police. Maybe you would like to sit down."

Maria was stunned. She could tell from the stern looks on the two men's faces that something was wrong. She sat down in the nearest chair and looked at the two with a look of bewilderment. She was expecting the worst.

Chief Brooks spoke up. "Mrs. Lee we have some bad news concerning your husband. We wanted to tell you first before you heard it on the news or from a friend. Your husband has been kidnapped by a couple of dope dealers. At this point, we don't know if he is dead or alive. When he was last seen he was alive. We want to assure you that we are doing everything in our power to get your husband back."

Chaplain George spoke up next. "I am here to provide you aid and comfort during this trial. Whatever you need you just let me know and I will see that you get it. If you want I will call any minister you know to come and assist you." Without hesitation, Maria blurted out, "Please call the bishop. His number is next to the kitchen phone."

Then Maria looked around and asked, "Where are the children?"

The Lee children had been oblivious to what was taking place. Their first indication that something was wrong was when a great big police officer came into the room and asked them to come with him to their living room. Their mother was sitting in an easy chair surrounded by men in blue uniforms. When the children appeared in the room, Maria broke down and began to cry. The oldest child, a boy, asked his mother what was wrong.

Maria was so overcome with emotion that she could only motion for the children to come to her. When the children got close, Maria, grabbed them and held on tight.

About then the doorbell rang. It was the Bishop, his wife, and the Relief Society President from Maria's church. Maria and her husband, Moreland, were Mormons. When an emergency arises in the Mormon Church, the Bishop is notified. It is the responsibility of the Bishop to take the necessary steps to assist any member in need. When Bishop Wilford Nielsen arrived at the Lee residence, he could see that there were a lot of people lending support to Maria. He, his wife and the Relief Society president were taken to Maria immediately. Maria was visibly upset but in control.

After the initial shock, Maria, had begun to get organized. With the arrival of the Bishop and Relief Society president, she could hand off some of the responsibility to them. Maria took the Bishop aside and asked if they could go somewhere quiet to say a prayer for her husband and her family. They found a room and knelt and prayed.

On the floor board of a car speeding down the interstate, a scared, tired, hungry and in pain police officer relaxed. A feeling that everything was going to be all right came over him. For the first time since this ordeal had begun, Officer Moreland Lee began to relax.

In his Homicide Office, Detective John Thomas was not so optimistic. He was now aware that the raid in West Seattle was not successful.

Chapter IX

The Search

Detective Thomas and his supervisors had gotten together. They decided that if they put the vehicle information out to the amber alert system that maybe they could alert Larry and Jeff to let them know they were being tracked. That way they would keep the officer alive to be used as a hostage if needed. Not a good scenario but the officer would be alive.

Larry and Jeff were pretty happy. They had secured enough money to keep them going for months. By then, they would be in another area and able to make money to keep them going for the rest of their lives.

Jeff was the first to pick up on the news that they were being tracked by the police, and were wanted for homicide and the kidnapping of a Seattle Police officer. He was cruising down Interstate Five nearing Olympia Washington. He was looking for a likely place to kill and dump the pig in back. He saw a traffic sign in front of him suddenly change from traffic information to amber alert information. As Jeff came closer to the sign he could read the information that had appeared on the sign. The sign had two parts. The first part read that Larry and Jeff were wanted for kidnapping a Seattle Police officer. The second part gave a description of their vehicle and license number. The sign asked that anybody with information contact the Seattle Police or nearest police organization by calling 911. Jeff was livid. How did the pigs get a description of this car? Must have been Jack or one of his bitches who gave the license to the pigs. Larry had been dozing when Jeff reached over and shook him awake.

"Wake up," said Jeff. "The pigs are looking for this car. We will have to ditch it." That got Larry's attention. He sat up immediately.

"How do you know?" asked Larry.

"There was a sign back there that had our names and a description of the car on it. Turn on the radio. Put it on KOMO 1000. That is the emergency radio for this area."

Larry tuned the radio to KOMO 1000 just in time to hear the announcer repeat the last message.

"This is an amber alert. Seattle Police are asking that you watch for a blue 2009 Ford thunderbird license ZMB2003 Washington plate. This vehicle is being driven by two white males named Larry Oliver and a Jeff Moore. They are accompanied by a white female Christy Copeland. All three are considered armed and dangerous. They are wanted in connection to four homicides and the kidnapping of a Seattle Police Officer. Do not approach these three. Call 911 if you see this car."

Larry swore under his breath. How did the pigs get the description of this vehicle? It was clean and never been stopped by the police. Larry surmised as did Jeff that it had to be Jack or one of his bitches who told. Larry made a mental note to kill Jack and his two whores the next time he ran into them.

Jeff was the observant one of the two as usual. He noted that he was travelling with three other cars. One was ahead, the other was alongside, but a third car was slightly behind and to his left. That car changed lanes which put him directly behind Jeff. The car also backed off a little. Jeff had a feeling that the driver of that car had read the same sign and was now reading the license plate on his vehicle. Jeff knew an exit was coming up that led to a shopping mall. He swerved across two lanes and took the exit. The other driver kept going.

Jeff was right, the other driver had picked up on the description and license of the car. He had his two children and his wife in his car. He was not about to follow the blue Thunderbird.

The driver got his cell phone out and called 911. About thirty minutes later information was relayed to Detective Thomas on the sighting. Detective Thomas at least knew the suspects were headed south. The question was whether they still had the officer.

The reaction to the sighting was instantaneous. Police units from several jurisdictions immediately flooded the area. Once again Larry and Jeff were able to escape the police dragnet. They drove to a nearby shopping mall. Once in the parking lot Jeff picked a row of cars on the outer edge of the mall parking area. These cars probably belonged to employees that worked at the mall and would not come out and find their car missing until after work. By then the three suspects would be gone and would have already stolen another vehicle at another location to cover their tracks.

Jeff guessed right. He found an older model vehicle which was easy to hotwire. The three suspects and the cop were put into this vehicle. Jane Elwood would come out and find her car missing. At first she felt she had just parked it somewhere other than where she thought she had parked it. She and a couple of fellow employees searched for a short time then reached the conclusion that the car had been stolen. Jane made a call to 911 to report the car missing. She was taken aback by the quick and almost overwhelming police response she got. Within minutes the mall parking lot was full of police units. It was not long before the blue thunderbird was found.

Jane had been listening to the police radio and heard the chatter going on. She quickly surmised that her vehicle had been stolen by a couple of dope dealers who had kidnapped a police officer. She was bursting to tell her husband. As soon as she was able, she called her husband on her cell phone to have him come and pick her up from work. At the same time, she told him the story of her missing car. Jim, Jane's husband, was a reporter for the local Olympia newspaper. He jumped into his car and sped to the mall.

Jim wasn't the only one who had picked up on the police radio transmissions. A young reporter who was out to make a name for himself had picked up on the radio transmissions. He too headed for the mall. By the time Jim got to the mall, the mall lot was filling up with TV and Radio newsmen. Jim was able to scoop them all. Jane was his wife.

By stealing the car, Jeff had bought the trio some much needed time. They were able to get to Centralia Washington. Larry was driving by then. Jeff was a passenger with "CC" in the back watching the pig.

The Rescue of the Officer Moreland Lee

Jeff spotted a tavern next to the freeway. He had Larry exit the freeway. They drove to the parking lot next to the freeway. Jeff decided to look inside the tavern before they decided which car to steal. He found a large group of people celebrating some event. He decided that this would be a good place to steal a car. No one would be coming out for a while. By then, they could be in Portland, Oregon where they would steal a car for the final leg of their journey to California. Once in California they would be safe. They could find a relatively secluded area to kill the pig, dump his body and be on their way.

Jeff once again picked an older model vehicle that was easy to hot wire. Once again they all piled into the vehicle and hit the road. Officer Lee was not sure was happening but he could sense that something was wrong. He had overheard Larry and Jeff talking about an amber alert sign. Then they got off the freeway and stole a car. If the car they were in was safe then why change cars and risk being seen by a citizen who would report the incident. Moreland had heard the police units go by as they got onto the freeway. He heard Larry and Jeff talk about a road block they had just missed on the freeway. Moreland deduced that the Washington State Patrol had literally shut the freeway down. Moreland knew that for the state patrol to take such an action there had to be something serious occurring. Now they were changing cars again. Obviously they were stealing this one too.

While Larry and Jeff were occupied, Moreland tried to reason with "CC". First, he tried to appeal to her feminine side. When that was rebuffed, he tried to reason with her intellectual side. That too was rebuffed. "CC" simply put a gun to Moreland's head and told him to shut up. In the end, Moreland decided he could not reason or bargain with "CC" so he lapsed into silence.

Jeff was getting sloppy. Instead of driving the stolen car to another location, he simply parked the car a few parking slots down from the car he was about to steal. Once again, they hit the freeway and headed south towards Portland, Oregon.

It took a couple of hours for Jason Kinnard to come out of the tavern and find his car missing. He got into an argument with his friends inside who felt he was too intoxicated to drive. One person offered to drive him home. Jason decided to call his girlfriend instead.

He elected to wait outside for her to arrive. As he exited the night club, he noticed an empty space where his car was parked. He figured that he had parked the car around the corner. He waited for his girlfriend to arrive before he went looking for the elusive car. Alcohol was affecting his ability to reason. He simply sat down on a bench infront of the night club and waited for his girlfriend.

Lisa, Jason's girlfriend, wasn't thrilled about coming after the drunken idiot. It wasn't the first time she had to go get him from one of his drunken binges. Someone must have taken his keys to keep him from driving. They would give them back in the morning when he got to work. She was going to see that he got up to go to work hangover and all. Besides if he did not make it to work, his boss would fire him.

As Lisa turned into the night club parking lot, she spotted Jason sitting on a bench in front of the club. At least, she wouldn't be embarrassed by having to go inside to get him.

As Lisa approached Jason, he looked up and stated, "My car is gone. I think someone has taken it." Lisa stopped for a second and looked at Jason. He was obviously drunk but seemed to be in control of his faculties.

"Where did you park it?" asked Lisa.

"I parked it right there," said Jason, pointing to an empty parking stall. "Let me look around," said Lisa. "I'll be right back."

Lisa shortly returned empty handed. She decided to go inside and ask the group if one of them had driven the car off. One person handed her the keys to the car, the rest denied any knowledge of the missing car. Lisa went back outside to tell Jason the bad news. "Jason,we need to call the police. Your car has been taken." Lisa took out her cell phone and called 911. The 911 operator took the information and instructed Lisa and Jason to wait in front of the club until a police unit would arrive to take the report. It was a warm evening with a cool breeze blowing so Lisa elected to sit down beside Jason and wait for the police.

It took deputy sheriff Mark Oler about twenty minutes to arrive at the club. He was met by Jason and his girlfriend Lisa. Jason, who was a little more composed approached the deputy. He stated, "My car is missing. I parked it over there," pointing to the empty spot.

Deputy Oler was a little skeptical considering Jason's inebriated state. He looked at Lisa, who appeared to be more alert and did not appear to be drinking.

Lisa spoke up and advised, "I have looked all over the lot and cannot find the car. I went inside and asked if anyone might have driven it off. The entire group denied any knowledge of the missing car. One person had taken Jason's keys to keep him from driving. That is all I have been able to determine."

On that basis, Deputy Oler decided that he should take a stolen report on the vehicle. He had spotted a car parked by itself in the lot and out of curiosity ran the plate on his terminal to see if he would get any hits. He then decided to speak to the group in the club to see if they knew anything. He would look to see if anything showed up in the computer on the plate he had ran later.

When an officer enters a plate into the system, his computer either goes to a local system first. Then it goes to a state system and finally on to a National Crime Information Center Maintained by the F.B.I. in Washington, D.C. If the car is stolen, it will pop up on the computer immediately. If there is a hazard associated with the plate, the computer will emit a low beeping sound and a red square will be activated and start flashing.

Deputy Oler had went inside the Club to talk to the patrons. He did not hear the beeping or see the red warning light. He had turned his radio down so he could hear the people in the bar. He did not hear his dispatch calling him either.

Rachel Gowen was sitting at her console reading. It was a slow night considering the time of night. It was mid-week so there wasn't a lot to do. She suddenly saw a red light start flashing on her monitor screen. She immediately dropped what she was doing to see what was going on.

Usually, when the red square lit up it meant that an officer's clipboard had hit the help the officer button on his console. A simple call to the officer would solve the problem. Rachel pulled up the information on the console. It showed that car 583 had run a plate that was stolen. There was a flag on the information indicating the occupants were armed and extremely dangerous. They were wanted in connection with a homicide and kidnapping of a police officer in Seattle Washington earlier in the day.

Rachel keyed her mike and called car 583 three times but did not get a response. Finally she pushed the override button to all units and stated:

"Attention all units, car 583 has run a plate which has come back stolen. The occupants of that vehicle are considered armed and extremely dangerous. They are wanted in connection to a Homicide that occurred in Seattle. These suspects have kidnapped a Seattle Police officer and may be holding him hostage. Car 583's last known location was outside Chehalis at the Red Duck night club taking a stolen car report. Car 583 is not answering his radio."

Deputy Oler was taken aback when he stepped out the door of the night club in time to see two police units with lights and sirens come screaming into the parking lot. He looked at the freeway and saw a steady stream of police cruisers with lights and sirens blaring coming down the freeway. He instinctively turned his radio up to see what was transpiring. By then the initial two police cruisers had come up to him. A Washington State Patrol trooper got out of his car and approached.

"You look okay. Are you all right?" asked the trooper. "Yeah, I'm fine. What is going on?"

"According to radio, you ran a plate on a car that came back stolen. The occupants are wanted for kidnapping a Seattle Police Office and homicide. You did not answer your radio when you were called."

Deputy Oler could see that the responding units were for him. Color drained from his face at first then his training took over.

"Call off those units before someone gets hurt and let me look and see what I have on my computer. The car I ran is over there," said Oler, pointing to a car parked off by itself.

Deputy Oler went to look at his computer information while other officers went to examine the stolen car. After verifying the information on the computer, Deputy Oler got out his cell phone and called dispatch. When someone answered he identified himself and asked to speak to Rachel Gowen. Rachel came on the phone right away.

"Hi Rachel, Mark Oler," said Deputy Oler.

Rachel responded, "Hi Mark. You had us worried there for a while. We couldn't raise you on the radio."

Deputy Oler sheepishly replied, "I am all right. Sorry about the mix up." "You are all right is all that matters," said Rachel.

Rachel and her husband had known Deputy Oler since he had graduated from high school. Deputy Oler and her husband had went fishing and hunting together.

"What is the story on the stolen car," asked Deputy Oler.

"Not sure yet, replied Rachel. I will make a call to the Seattle Police homicide office and get back to you."

"Ok," replied Deputy Oler. "I will need an impound for the car. We will go talk to the patrons in the club and see if anyone knows anything. I will call you back when we are done."

The patrons at the nightclub became aware that something was afoot when the whole place was suddenly flooded with police officers. One patron decided he did not like the police and stood up to protest the action. He found himself lying face down on the floor before he could finish his sentence. Everyone else looked at the grim faces of the officers and decided now was not the time for obstruction or insolence toward the police. The officers quickly decided that no one was involved with the car in the parking lot. As quickly as they had come the officers left with the smart ass in tow.

Rachel had been busy, upon hanging up with Deputy Oler. She immediately placed a phone call to the Seattle Police Homicide unit. She was connected to a detective Thomas. Detective Thomas had given up on the search for Officer Lee and was about to go home when the call from Rachel came in.

"Is this the detective in charge of the kidnapping of the police officer?" asked Rachel.

"It is, replied Detective Thomas, and who might you be?"

"I am Rachel Gowen chief dispatcher from Lewis County Washington by Chehalis, Washington. We have found a car listed as stolen out of Olympia Washington. The hit indicates the vehicle was being used in a homicide and a kidnapping of a Seattle Police officer. The information indicates we should contact you if the car is located".

"Was the vehicle occupied?" asked Detective Thomas.

"No such luck, stated Rachel. However we were sent on a stolen car report at the same location. I wonder if there is a connection."

"That is the MO they used in Olympia. They ditched the car they were in and stole another car. They picked a car that they felt would not be missed for a while. They have about a four hour head start," replied Thomas.

"Okay, we will impound this car with a hold for you. We can process the car for prints and DNA if you want. We can expedite the request. It would mean getting someone from the state crime lab down here to process it."

"Let's do it," stated Thomas. I assume you will enter the information on the stolen car into NCIC with a flag and a notation on the kidnapping."

"We will and good luck," stated Rachel.

Rachel hung up from the phone with Detective Thomas and immediately dialed Ted Daugherty of the state crime lab.

"When Ted answered the phone, Rachel stated, sorry to wake you Ted but we need a vehicle processed ASAP. We believe it was used in the kidnapping of a police officer from Seattle and is driven by a couple of bad ass drug dealers wanted for homicide."

When Rachel said the kidnapping of a police officer, Ted immediately became alert. Ted's whole family had a law enforcement background. Both his older brother and sister were in the F.B.I. His father and uncle were both retired from the Washington State Patrol. Ted was eager to help any way he could. It took Ted about three hours to process the vehicle and establish that fingerprints found in the car belonged to Larry, Jeff and Christy "CC" Copeland. DNA found on the backseat came back to Officer Moreland Lee. The DNA evidence showed that the officer was still alive up to that point.

When Detective Thomas heard the news he breathed a sigh of relief. He knew it was going to be a long night. Thomas decided to let the family of Officer Lee know about the progress of the case.

As soon as the phone rang at the Lee home, the phone was picked up and a voice stated, "Lee residence."

"This is detective Thomas of the Seattle Police Homicide. Is Mrs. Lee there?" "One moment please," said the voice on the other end of the line.

Shortly, a very shaken and upset voice came on the line. It was a female voice who seemed to be very tired and shook up. "This is Mrs. Lee," stated the voice. Maria, was fearing the worse as she answered.

"Mrs. Lee, this is Detective Thomas from the Seattle Police Homicide office. I hope I haven't upset you. I just wanted you to know what we have learned so far. We have tracked the people who took your husband to around Chehalis Washington. Forensic evidence at this point suggests your husband is still alive. I hope that makes you feel better."

Detective Thomas could hear the phone drop and a person seemed to fall to the floor. He heard someone ask if she was all right. He heard someone exclaim, "He's alive! He's alive!" then came sobbing. Presently someone picked the phone up. "May I ask who this is?" said the voice on the other end.

Detective Thomas identified himself and recounted what he had learned from the dispatcher in Lewis County. The voice on the other end thanked him for the update and hung the phone up. Detective Thomas wondered just how long the officer was going to survive.

Chapter X

The Security guard

Larry and Jeff were starting to breathe easier. They had made it south to the Oregon border without any problems. They seemed to have out run the police dragnet. Once in Oregon they would steal another car and head down highway 101.

Jeff knew Portland quite well. He decided to take the Lombard exit once they entered Oregon and got off the bridge that spans the Columbia River between Washington and Oregon. Jeff knew of several used car lots along Lombard. They would pick one out and steal a car from the lot.

It wasn't long before Jeff had found a lot and a car that looked good to him. Larry and he took the officer out of the car and put him into the car they were going to steal. Jeff parked the car they had taken from near Chehalis Washington and parked it on the side of the road next to the lot. Jeff figured that by the time the theft was discovered they would be in California. Once there, they could rent a legitimate car and abandoned the stolen car. By then, they would have killed the officer and left him where his body would not be found for some time. Jeff did not figure on Ronald Ackerman, a security officer.

Ronald Ackerman was what police professionals called a "wanna be" police officer. Ron had taken tests and appeared before oral boards in an attempt to secure a position with a police department. So far he had had no luck. He secured a position with a local security firm. His duties were to drive around after business hours and check businesses to insure there were no break ins or thefts. Part of Ronald's duties was to patrol around the car lots on Lombard Street in North Portland.

He had found a decent looking car on a lot that he patrolled. Ron had come in on his time off and made inquiries about the car. He had learned the price of the car and mileage from the manager of the lot. Ron told the manager that he was interested in the car but still needed some more money in order to make the down payment. An arrangement was made with the manager that allowed Ron to put some money down. In exchange, the manager would hold the vehicle until Ron could scrape up enough money to make the down payment. It was a win win for the manager. He knew he would make a sale plus he knew Ron would give extra attention to his lot since he had an interest in one of the cars on the lot.

It was a slow night for security officer Ackerman. There was not much to do. His paperwork was caught up. His equipment had been cleaned and updated. He had driven by the car lot earlier to check on his favorite car. His car lot check was over so he went on a coffee break before he had to start his rounds again. Things were looking up for Ron. He had been told that the security company had decided to promote him to sergeant. That would mean he would get a small raise and could afford to buy his car sooner. Ron turned onto Lombard and headed south. This route would take him by the car lot where his car was parked. He could check on it as he drove by on his way to another car lot he was tasked with checking. To his surprise, the car was not parked in its usual spot. Ron noted that there was an empty spot where the car had been. He decided to check the lot to see if someone had moved the care since he was last there earlier in the evening. A check of the lot did not find the car. Ron noted that there was a car parked on the street close to where his car had been parked. He made a mental note of the car and reached for his cell phone.

"911, what is your emergency," said the operator on the other end of the line.

"My name is Ron Ackerman. I am a security officer for Pacific Security. I am at a car lot in the 7900 Block of Lombard Ave. I think there is a car that has been stolen off the lot."

"You say your name is Ron Ackerman and you work for Pacific Security?" "Yes."

"How do you know the car is stolen?'

"The car in question is a car I am interested in buying. I have an arrangement with the manager of the lot so that I can make payments on the car. I came by earlier today and the car was there. I just drove by and the car is missing. There is an empty space in the line where the car had been parked and it is gone."

"I will send an officer out to investigate. Where can we locate you once we get there?"

"I will be in a blue marked security car parked in front of the lot," responded Ron.

After answering a couple of questions, Ron hung his phone up. He settled in to wait for the arrival of the police officer. He had a book written by a Joseph Wambaugh entitled, "The Onion Field." He had just finished a couple of pages when a squad car driven by a Carl Yamamoto arrived.

Ron got out of his vehicle and approached the officer as he got out of his vehicle.

"Hi, I am Ron Ackerman, the one who called this in. The car in question was parked over there," stated Ron, pointing to an empty slot where the car had been parked.

"I am Carl Yamamoto," replied the officer. "Do we have a contact number for the owner of the lot so we can contact him?" asked Officer Yamamoto. "I have it right here," replied Ron.

Officer Yamamoto took the number and called the owner which turned out to be the manager. After a short conversation, Officer Yamamoto hung up.

He turned to Ron and stated, "The manager will be here shortly."

Ron replied, "Okay, while we are waiting, you might want to check out that car sitting a few doors down. It is strange that it is parked there. No one is around and all the businesses in this area are closed for the night. Plus it has Washington plates on it."

As a matter of routine, Officer Yamamoto ran the plate more to satisfy Ron than for any other reason. Both men then stood and waited for the car lot manager to arrive.

Officer Yamamoto was startled when a code was broadcast over the air with his car designation.

Officer Yamamoto replied, "Go ahead radio."

"Car 2 David 5, that plate you just ran is associated with a homicide and the kidnapping of a Seattle Police officer. Its occupants are considered armed and extremely dangerous. Officer Yamamoto instantly replied, "I will be standing by in the 7900 block of Lombard."

That statement sent a message to other units that the officer was not sure what he had and was requesting other units to back him up until he knew what was happening.

Officer Yamamoto then turned to Ron and ordered him to move closer to his police car. Ron was not sure what was occurring but looking at the expression on Officer Yamamoto's face he knew something was afoot.

Lombard Avenue is fairly flat and cars can be seen coming for some distance. To Yamamoto it seemed like an eternity before units responded to his call for assistance. As he waited he could see up and down Lombard. It seemed like a sea of blue suddenly erupted. Police cars with their blue lights on were coming from both directions. Within seconds the first unit arrived.

Officer Yamamoto approached the first unit and stated, "The car is over there," pointing to the parked car. "It is unoccupied, I don't know if the suspects are still in the area. It looks like the suspects could have abandoned the stolen vehicle and took another car off this lot. We had better search the area just in case."

By then, the shift supervisor had arrived named Sgt. Poindexter. Poindexter listen to Ron and Officer Yamamoto. Ron related the story of the car to Sgt. Poindexter. Officer Yamamoto filled him in on being dispatched to investigate a possible stolen vehicle. He related how he had ran the plate of the suspect vehicle at the insistence of Ron. That was how the incident went up to that point.

Sgt. Poindexter got on the radio and asked for an ETA on the car lot manager.

Radio advised that the manager lived close by and should be arriving momentarily. Just as Sgt. Poindexter got off the radio the manager pulled into the lot. Averil Roberts was surprised at the number of police cars around his car lot. He got out of his vehicle with a look of astonishment on his face. His bewildered look did not last long. He was approached by an older police officer with stripes on his sleeves. Sgt. Poindexter spoke first.

"Are you the owner here?"

"I am the manager. A conglomerate from out of state is the real owners."

"We have a report that one of your cars has been stolen. It was parked there" said Poindexter pointing to the empty space. "This is where the car was parked and this is the person reporting the theft," said Poindexter pointing to Ron Ackerman.

Averil instantly recognized Ron. Averil asked Ron what had happened. Ron repeated the Story to Averil, including the part about the car sitting three doors down being used in the kidnapping of a Seattle Police Officer.

"That was your favorite car, wasn't it?" asked Averil. "Yes it was," replied Ron.

Averil turned to Sgt. Poindexter and stated, "Let's go into my office and look up the paperwork".

At that point, Averil, Ron, Sgt. Poindexter and Officer Yamamoto went to the car lot office. Averil opened the door and let the trio in. He went to a file cabinet and opened a drawer. He took out a folder that had the picture and information on the car.

Officer Yamamoto took the folder and copied the information onto a police report. Officer Yamamoto had Averil sign the report which indicated that the report was true and accurate.

Upon completion of the report, police radio was notified that a signed stolen report had been made. Poindexter also asked radio to notify the Seattle Police Homicide unit of the stolen car and subsequent theft of another vehicle.

Chapter XI

Sarah and Melissa

Sarah Caldwell was tasked with the need to enter the stolen car into the computer system. First, she decided to call the Seattle Police Homicide and see what they wanted to do with the recovered car and any other instructions the Homicide Unit had.

Sarah dialed the number. A rather tired and grumpy voice on the other end of the phone stated, "Seattle Police Homicide, Detective Thomas."

Sarah identified herself and briefly outlined what had happened in Portland.

Detective Thomas was no longer grumpy and tired, he was very much alert and engaged.

He began to issue orders to Sarah. "First, have you impounded the vehicle?" asked Thomas.

"We have a tow truck on the way," responded Sarah.

"Good. Don't let any one touch the vehicle any more than they have to. We need to establish that Officer Lee was in the vehicle and he was still alive. Do you see any blood in the back seat and particularly in the floor board in the back?"

"I don't know. Let me ask."

Sarah keyed up her microphone and called to Sgt. Poindexter.

When Poindexter answered, she asked. "Do you see any blood on the rear seat or floorboard?"

Poindexter replied, "Stand by radio, I will check." Poindexter came back shortly and stated, "There seems to be some blood spots on the floor and part of the seat, nothing significant."

Sarah then turned to the phone and stated, "There are some blood spots but nothing significant."

"Good," replied Thomas. "Have your crime tech people take blood samples. I will send you DNA info to compare the blood to."

Sarah then turned her attention to the communications sheet she was preparing. She took the sheet and went to the teletype office. It read:

To: All west coast police agencies
From: Portland Police Headquarters / Multnomah County Sheriff
Subject: Recovered Stolen Car Used in Homicide

On this date, the Portland Police has recovered a stolen car believed to be used in a homicide getaway in the Seattle area. Additionally, it is believed the occupants of the vehicle kidnapped a Seattle Police Officer and is holding him hostage. The occupants are believed to be a Larry Oliver, a Jeff Moore, and a Christy Copeland. All suspects are considered armed and extremely dangerous.

These three may have stolen a nearby vehicle off a car lot. That vehicle is described as an apple red 1997 Chevrolet 4 door Oregon license plate XAB555. If this vehicle is found or seen approach with extreme caution. The plate has been entered into NCIC as a stolen vehicle. EOM Melissa Farwell, who took the sheet, was taken aback when she read the contents.

She knew that a police officer's life hung in the balance. She decided to take some extraordinary actions to see that as many people were notified as possible.

Melissa was not a member of the police family. Her first contact with a police officer was through the D.A.R.E. program which was an anti – drug program taught in schools. She was nine years old at the time. She was impressed with the crisp clean uniform of the officer who taught the class. To her, he was larger than life. She had decided that she wanted to be a part of the police family. As she grew up she began to read up on police procedure and read books on the police experience. By the time, she graduated from high school she was pretty set on becoming a police officer. In college, she took courses in criminal justice and graduated with a degree in criminal science. She took time off from her studies to work for a while. She had applied at the Multnomah county dispatch office. To her surprise, she was hired.

Melissa had to be sure that as many people as possible had to get the message about this vehicle. Melissa put the message out over the teletype system immediately. Then, she took an extra step she knew of.

Melissa picked up the phone, and called an old friend she had went to school with. His name was Jim Foster who was the local head of a group called "React." React was a nationwide CB club that assisted the police with minor emergencies. They acted as the eyes and ears of the police when needed.

When the phone rang a very sleepy and tired Jim Foster picked up the phone and said, "Hello."

"Jim, this is Melissa Farwell at the sheriff's office dispatch center. I hate to wake you but we have an emergency here at the sheriff's office and I need your help."

Jim replied, "Sure, whats up."

Melissa recounted the story of the Seattle homicide to Jim and the stolen vehicle in Portland. By then, Jim was wide awake. He and Melissa had been in high school together. He didn't know she was working in police dispatch for the county. Her story was incredible.

Jim interrupted Melissa for a moment and stated, "hold on a second while I get to the other room and a note pad I can write on". Jim came back on the phone almost immediately and said," let me make sure I have this right. A cop was kidnapped in Seattle. The cops have traced a series of stolen cars to the Portland area. The police are now looking for that vehicle in Oregon. It is believed that the kidnappers are headed for California with the officer as a hostage."

"That is the problem in a nutshell," stated Melissa. "Can you help?" "Jim replied immediately," you bet, give me a second to turn my equipment on."

Within a matter of seconds the information on the suspect vehicle was being broadcast to every base station, long hauler, camper and hunter with a CB radio tuned to one of two channels nine and nineteen.

When Melissa heard the info being broadcast she breathed a sigh of relief. She knew that somewhere someone would hear the broadcast and see the vehicle. It was just a matter of time.

Chapter XII

The Old Man on the Mountain

James Davis Had built a house on a mountain with his wife, Laura. They had lived some wonderful years on that mountain top. You could sit on their front porch and watch the wild game graze and play off their porch. It was idyllic.

Their grandchildren would come and visit. It was fun watching the various types of wildlife play in their front yard. The animals had a sense of security here. They instinctively knew that they were safe from the hunters here.

One year, a group of hunters stumbled onto the place. Jim had seen them come in and knew they did not have permission to be there. In a rage he went down to where the hunters were and told them to leave in no uncertain terms. The hunters were so taken aback by this old guy that they apologized immediately and left.

Their Garden of Eden came to an end when Laura was diagnosed with terminal cancer. One minute, she was there and the next minute she was gone. Her death devastated Jim. He became a loner, and withdrew from society for a time.

Jim was sitting on his front porch one day just staring off into space. He was feeling sorry for himself and not paying attention to anything in particular when he suddenly became aware of someone on the road below his house. Someone was staggering up the road as if he was drunk.

Jim had no tolerance for drunks. His first thought was how did a drunk get onto his road and what did he want. Jim started to stare at the stranger. He suddenly got the feeling that this was not a drunk. The stranger kept coming very slowly. Jim began to realize that this man needed help and was trying to reach his home. Jim got up off his porch and started down the road. Just as he did the stranger collapsed in the roadway. Jim began to walk faster. He could see the man was trying to get up. Just as Jim got to him the stranger was able to stand. He immediately collapsed into Jim's arms.

Jim recognized immediately that the man was going into shock and was overheated. Jim took him to his patio and laid him down. He took his water hose and began to spray the man down. Next he got a glass of water and had the man take a few sips. Jim wouldn't allow the man to drink it all at once. Once the man was able to speak, Jim, asked him what he was doing in the woods and on foot. The man whose name was "Don" told Jim an incredible story.

It seemed that Don and his family had decided to leave the main road and go into the woods to look for mushrooms. They drove up this old logging road and eventually got high centered in their vehicle. For the first day and a half, they had tried to get the car unstuck and turned around. By the end of the second day, they realized they were stuck and needed help getting out. It was terribly hot and they were out of water. Alice, one of the children, had seen a glint of something shining through the trees. Whatever it was, was high up the mountain.

Don was the father and it was his job to go find help. Don started out in the early morning so there was not much sun to put up with while he went searching for help. Don had not counted on the thickness of the brush and the heat. By the time he was able to reach the road that led to Jim's property, he was exhausted. The knowledge that his family were depending on him kept him going. Don's shirt was wringing wet with sweat. By the time Don caught sight of Jim's home, he had become disoriented and could hardly stand. He was aware that he had fallen and was just barely able to get up. Just as he got to his feet, he again started to collapse. Somehow he had fallen into someone's arms. He was just barely conscious as he was half dragged and half carried up the hill. Don started to come to as the cool water from the water hose was sprayed on him. He eventually came to enough to tell the stranger helping him about his family. The stranger excused himself and went into the house.

Jim immediately called 911. When the call taker answered the phone, Jim relayed what the stranger had told him. It took about forty five minutes for a deputy sheriff to arrive. Don told the sheriff what happened and approximately where the family was located. A local search and rescue team were the first to find the family. They were alive but suffering from heat exhaustion.

All of the family were taken to the main road and evacuated by helicopter to a nearby hospital where they were treated and released within a few hours except Don who was kept overnight for observation.

This man's plight gave Jim an idea. He could set up a base station in the mountains and monitor it for emergencies. Jim went about investigating the whole situation. He bought equipment to install in his home. He contacted the local sheriff's office and asked them what equipment they need to set up a base camp for search and rescue. Once he got the list of equipment needed, he simply went out and bought it. He had a radio tower installed in his front yard. He contacted the local React organization and obtained a React number. He was designated React 59. Finally, he contacted the local search and rescue chairman and let him know what equipment was available to him. Jim invited Greg Foreman to come and test the equipment. Greg took him up on the offer and came to see what Jim was talking about.

Greg came and tested the equipment. He was satisfied with the set up. In fact some of the equipment had state of the art attachments that Greg only dreamed of owning.

It wasn't long before Greg had the chance to test out the new system, a couple who went missing while hiking was reported to search and rescue. It took about two days to find the lost couple.

During the search, Jim's home became headquarters for the search effort. Search and rescue personnel could come and rest or get orders for the next area to search.

It wasn't long before Jim's place became the choice point for rescue operations. He had a trailer house brought into the property and converted it to a five bedroom unit complete with a kitchen for cooking and a shower. When it was not in use Jim, kept it locked up.

One time his search and rescue efforts came to the attention of the civil air patrol. Jim found himself flooded with CAP personnel. His trailer house was full and people were sleeping on the couch in his basement. After a week the downed aircraft was spotted. All in the craft were dead.

Jim was about to go to bed one night when he heard the hostage report come over the air. He wrote the info on a note pad that he kept in the radio room. He turned off the lights and was about to go to sleep when he heard the familiar call on channel nine. "Breaker. Breaker. Does anyone hear this transmission."

Chapter XIII

The Sighting

Larry and Jeff were feeling pretty good about themselves. They had left the Portland area without any police involvement. After a few miles, both felt it was time to get rid of the pig in the back seat. Larry was driving so it fell upon him to find a quiet place to kill the cop and dump the body. There were a few places to dump the body but there was always some house in the way. After a few miles, Larry found what looked like a good spot. He turned in and went in a few yards only to find a family and a camper already there. Larry swore under his breath and turned around to get back onto the main road.

Jeff was already agitated. He wanted to be rid of this cop as well. He felt that they had let him live too long as it was.

Officer Moreland Lee was devastated. From the conversation he had gathered from the two suspects in the front seat, he knew that his end was near. It was just a matter of finding the right spot. His attempt to reach "CC" had failed. She was just as hard core as the two males. Moreland knew that his only chance was to run once he was let out of the car. He knew that his survival rate was fifty - fifty once he was out of the vehicle and running. Victims had survived this scenario. He knew that he was going to be shot. The question was, was the wound going to be fatal? He didn't seem to have any other choice. Christy on the other hand just wanted it over. She had baby sat this cop since the beginning. At one point, the cop had tried to appeal to her maternal instincts. That failed. She simply kicked him in the side and told him to shut the fuck up. She thought about shooting this pig herself but something inside her told her not to do it. When

The Rescue of the Officer Moreland Lee

Larry found a suitable side road she thought it was finally over. She was thoroughly piqued when she saw the camper and family. This just meant that she would have to spend more time with this pig. "CC" was so pissed that she hardly noticed the semi as they exited onto the main road. The semi was driven by a Bill (Squawman) Knight. He got the nickname because he had been married to an Indian woman named Jeannette Little Wolf. Jeannette was good looking and a real babe. She and Bill had run a small business in Gresham, Oregon. Both were happy and enjoyed life.

Jeannette was coming down the highway one day early in the morning on her way to work. She was happy and excited. The doctor had told her the day before that she was pregnant. She couldn't wait for Bill to get home from visiting relatives so she could tell him the good news.

A car coming in the opposite direction suddenly lost control and took Jeannette head on. Jeannette was killed instantly. The other driver was a drunk. He lived.

Bill was devastated. For weeks, he lived in a fog of misery. Finally, he decided that he must move on. Bill decided that he could drive truck and see and talk with people until the hurt went away.

An enterprising driver had seen Jennie picture lying on a table, while Bill was using the shower facilities at a truck stop. He posted the picture on the internet. It wasn't long before the picture went viral. Every trucker learned who Bill and Jenny were. She became a celebrity.

Bill had met Ralph Wiggens on one of his runs from Portland, Oregon to Los Angeles. They hit it off immediately. Ralph was driving for a company. Bill was an independent contractor who was working for himself. It didn't take Ralph long to figure out that this was the husband of Jennie who was the talk of the circuit. It didn't take him long either to figure out that Jennie was dead. Nor did it take him long to figure out why Bill was driving truck.

Ralph took it upon himself to alert the other drivers that Jenny was dead and to stop sending messages about her. Instead of stopping the gossip, Ralph created a guardian angel. Each trucker that knew about Jenny came to call her the guardian angel of truckers.

Bill was oblivious to what was going on. He finally found out from a half tipsy driver at a stop one night when the individual approached Bill and wanted to shake his hand and express his condolences.

The encounter brought tears to Bill's eyes. He had thought that no one would remember Jennie. He took the words of the driver to heart.

Bill and Ralph had hooked up in Portland. Both were headed for Los Angeles. Bill had a load and Ralph was deadheading back to L.A. They had decided to keep each other company.

Bill was slow because he had a load. Ralph had gotten a few miles ahead of Bill. Both were communicating via CB radio. Both heard the broadcast about the stolen car and the hostage situation. The alert was simple and short, "To all units listening to this channel, this is an alert issued by the Oregon State Police. They are looking for a red 1997 Chevrolet 4dr. lic. XAB555. This vehicle is believed to be involved in the kidnapping of a Seattle police officer and several homicides that occurred in the Seattle area. Any person coming into contact with this vehicle or its occupants are asked to notify your local 911. Do not approach these people as they are considered armed and extremely dangerous."

"Did you hear that?" asked Bill.

"Sounds like some cop has got his tit in a wringer," replied Ralph.

Ralph wasn't real fond of the police. He had gotten a couple of tickets recently and was not too happy with the police. Bill on the other hand held no such animus toward the police.

When Ralph told him about the tickets, Bill simply told him to pay the damn things and get on with his life.

Ralph was talking about his last hunting trip when Bill interrupted him.

"Ralph, that car the Oregon State Police is looking for just pulled out in front me a couple of seconds ago. It is headed your way".

For a second, Ralph was taken aback. Then he came back', "Are you sure?"

"Yeah," replied Bill. "The license plate number is the same. We will have to notify someone. My cell phone shows no service. How about yours?" "Mine shows no service as well," replied Ralph. "There is an old man on the mountain near here. Why don't you try him? He usually monitors channel nine this time of night."

The Rescue of the Officer Moreland Lee

"Stand by, let me see if I can raise someone on that channel". "Breaker nine, breaker nine this is squaw man, does anyone hear this channel?" Bill waited a few seconds then tried again, "Breaker nine, breaker nine, does anyone hear this channel?" This time the answer was almost instantaneous. "This is React 59 over," came the calm crisp response.

"This is squaw man. I am on route 219 headed down to route 595 to get onto HiWay 101 to California. Someone broadcast a request to locate a red car with Oregon plates XAB555 a few minutes ago. That car is in front of me about a quarter of a mile. Do you have the ability to call the authorities and alert them of the location?"

Jim Davis had heard a number of calls on channel nine through the months.

Mostly they were lost people or pets. This was the first time he had encountered such a call. His first reaction was one of stunned disbelief. It took a couple of seconds for him to regain his composure. Then he began to react to the caller.

"Describe the car to me," requested Jim.

"It is a red late 90's Chevrolet license XAB555," replied Bill. "Standby, while I call this in," said Jim.

Jim reached over and picked up his phone. He dialed 911 expecting a short delay.

To his surprise, the phone was answered within a couple of rings. "911 operator 15 what is your emergency?" "Debbie, this is Jim Davis. Is this you?" asked Jim.

"It sure is, Jim. How is it going? I wish I was up there with you. My kids and their noise is driving me nuts."

Jim started to laugh but caught himself. Tonight he had a real crisis he needed to report.

"Debbie, you are welcome to come up anytime you want but I have a bigger issue at the moment. You know that red Chevrolet with that officer hostage. It has been sighted by a truck driver on route 219 near the intersection with route 595. It looks like they are near the town of Agness."

It took Debbie a second to digest what Jim had just told her. Then her training kicked in. She asked Jim to repeat the information as he had gotten it from the trucker. Once she had verified the information she asked Jim how to contact the driver. Jim gave her the CB channel he was on. After Jim had told her all the information he hung up. He knew that Debbie would call him back if she needed him or to just let him know what happened.

It seemed like an eternity to Bill Knight before anyone got back to him. Bill had been expecting Jim to re - contact him. Instead a cold female voice came over channel nine.

"This is operator fifteen at the county sheriff's dispatch center does a Bill "Squaw man" Knight hear this channel?"

Bill picked up his mike and responded, "This is Squaw man over."

"This is the dispatch center for the county sheriff. We are getting a report that you have that red Chevy License XAB555 in sight. Is that correct"? "Yes maam, replied Bill, when he came out of that side road I almost ran him over. These idiots don't seem to understand that you can't stop these rigs on a dime".

"Are you able to tell me what mile post you are at", inquired Debbie? "I am at mile post 123 on state route 219"."

"Are you still able to see the car in question?"

"Yes, Maam. but I am losing sight of him. I have a full load and am slowing down. I do have a friend ahead of me who is dead heading. He may be able to pick them shortly."

"Don't you guys be heros. Just keep them in sight until I can get some help."

After Debbie left, Bill went back to channel nineteen to tell Ralph what was going on. Ralph listened to what Bill had to say. Then, Ralph came up with a plan. Ralph would take his truck and place it across the road just outside of the town of Agness creating a natural barrier. Bill would come up behind the vehicle and put his truck across the road creating a barrier that would prevent the three suspects from getting into town or escaping. All of this would depend on the 911 operator getting some help there.

Chapter XIV

Posse

Debbie in dispatch had a problem; she had no units available. On any other day it would not have been a problem. Tonight, the problem was that the main state patrol unit was tied up on an injury accident involving a possible death. The local sheriff and one of his deputies were on a drug bust in another part of the county. The remaining deputy was on an out of state extradition Warrant and wouldn't be back until the next day. There was one state trooper who was twenty five miles away. Debbie calculated that trooper could catch the suspect vehicle just about Agness Oregon if he pushed it. The only problem was this was a one man car and what would happen once the car caught up with the suspects.

Debbie would have to deal with the problem as it developed. She keyed her mike and called "unit 509." She did not get an immediate response. She tried again, "unit 509." She still did not get a response. She tried a third time, "Unit 509, do you hear radio". This time she heard the crisp reply of trooper Jackson, "This is unit 509."

"509, can you start for the vicinity of Agness Oregon. We have a report of a sighting of the car wanted in a homicide and the kidnapping of a Seattle Police Officer. The occupants of that vehicle are considered armed and extremely dangerous. Do not approach this vehicle by yourself." "Received," replied 509.

The DUI suspect in the trooper's back seat was stunned when the trooper opened the back door of the cruiser and ordered him out. Trooper Jackson told the man to not drive drunk again, then, the trooper jumped into his cruiser and sped off.

Debbie in the meantime had to figure out how to get help for trooper Jackson. Her resources were limited. She picked up the phone and called Mitch Connors who was the local town constable and part time deputy in Agness. The phone rang for what seemed like an eternity, finally a sleepy voice answered the phone.

"Hello," said the sleepy voice.

"Is this Mitch Connors?" asked Debbie.

"It is," replied Mitch, who began to sense this was not an ordinary call. "Officer Connors, this is the sheriff's dispatch center calling. We have a report that a car wanted in a homicide and the kidnapping of a Seattle Police Officer is headed your way. We have a one man car headed your way to intercept the suspect vehicle. The officer will need some assistance. We estimate the officer will make contact right around Agness. Would you be available to assist?" They should arrive at your location in about an hour.

Mitch had received many calls to assist deputy sheriffs but nothing like this. It took a second to digest what the dispatcher was saying. He was now wide awake and sat up in bed. His sudden movement woke his wife Darlene up.

"What is wrong?" she asked.

"Nothing," replied Mitch. "Go back to sleep."

Mitch got out of bed and started talking to the dispatch center. He headed for the closet where he kept his uniform and gun. He informed the dispatcher that he could call his brother in law to assist. His brother in law had been a sniper in Vietnam. That would make three people to intercept the vehicle. Debbie the dispatcher also told Mitch that two semi truckers had volunteered to block the roadway to stop the suspect vehicle from getting away. Mitch hung up the phone then called his brother in law who was not thrilled at getting a call from Mitch so late at night. Once Mitch explained to his brother in law what had happened, he was ready to go.

Gary, the brother-in-law, had been a sniper in Vietnam. He had come home, got a job and led a peaceful life. He had raised a couple of children who had blessed him with grandchildren. He did not discuss Vietnam with anyone, If you had not known Gary for a long time, you would not even have known he was in the war.

One time, Gary had taken a grandchild camping with him. The grandchild had wandered off. After a couple of hours, Gary, got worried and started to search for the child. It wasn't long before the grandchild wandered back into camp. Gary was beside himself. When Gary started to scold him, the grandchild looked at him and said, "Grandpa you taught me how to read a compass".

Gary had Mitch pick up his hunting partner whom Gary, had alerted as well. The three of them proceeded to an area that was ideal for the stop. Just as they arrived the first semi was seen coming down the road. Mitch positioned his vehicle on the roadway to let the truck through in case he was not the one the dispatcher had told him about.

Shortly the semi pulled up next to Mitch. The driver yelled out the window, "Are you the one needing the road blocked?"

"Yeah," replied Mitch.

"Where do you want me?" asked Ralph.

"Put it across here but leave me enough room to let traffic through," said Mitch.

As Ralph was parking, the truck the headlights from the suspect vehicle appeared on the mountain top.

"We haven't got a lot of time before they get here," observed Ralph.

"Are you alone?" asked Ralph. He didn't see anyone else around. "No," replied Mitch. "There are two snipers hidden in the brush nearby."

As the suspect vehicle got to the bottom of the hill, the lights of another semi emerged behind him. Within seconds the blue lights of a police cruiser emerged as well. Within a matter of minutes the whole group would come through town and run into the roadblock. Mitch and Ralph ducked behind the constable's car and got ready. Ralph had retrieved his pistol from the cab of his truck and hunkered down ready for whatever awaited him. Mitch was just glad that the trucker was willing to join the fray.

Trooper Carlos Villa had been monitoring the transmissions from the adjoining sector. He was not too far from where the events were occurring. He picked up his mike and advised radio that he was not too far away and would head in that direction. He cut down the bypass at Ophit and hit route 595 near Bognal Ferry. He then turned northwest on 595 which would take him straight into Agness. He just prayed that he would get there in time.

Chapter XV

The Final Stand

Larry and Jeff were feeling pretty good about themselves. They had eluded the pigs and were nearing the California line. In fact, the closer they got to the border the more they wanted to celebrate. It was in such a mood that they came around the curve and spotted the road block.

At first, Jeff was furious then the cold calculating mind of a psychopath took over. His only thought was to figure a way out of his predicament. He turned around to look and see if they could go back to the little town they had just come through. He saw a semi turning crossways in the road blocking their escape. Jeff then looked forward again. He saw the police cruiser driven by trooper Villa coming up the road with his lights flashing.

Larry had pulled his car within fifty yards of the makeshift roadblock. He had stopped to make an assessment of their situation.

CC was in the backseat. She had turned to look out the back window. She exclaimed very loudly, "Look up the mountain!" She saw the flashing lights of the police cruiser driven by trooper Jackson as it neared the roadblock. CC had a sense of foreboding and burst into tears.

She dropped her pistol and crumbled into a mass of jelly.

For the first time in his long ordeal, Officer Lee began to sense a feeling of relief. He struggled to get a view of the situation. Just then Jeff appeared over the top of the seat and snarled, "You fucking pig. You are the cause of all this." Jeff managed to point his gun at Officer Lee when his head literally exploded. Blood, hair, and bone went in

The Rescue of the Officer Moreland Lee

every direction. Blood started to pour out of the torso where Jeff's head had been. Officer Lee had to force himself off the floorboard and onto the back seat to escape the blood flow. He could hear CC screaming at the top of her lungs.

Gary, the Vietnam sniper understood the orders given by Mitch. He was not to fire unless the life of the hostage was threatened. When Jeff looked over the back seat and pointed the gun at Officer Lee that was enough for Gary. He squeezed off a shot that hit Jeff square in the head.

Larry saw what had happened to Jeff. Instead of making him want to surrender, it just infuriated him. Larry got out of the car screaming, "Come on you bastards. You want to shoot me then shoot!" Larry then began to shoot at Mitch, Ralph and the newly arrived trooper Villa. Gary could not get a clear shot at Larry.

Bill could not get a chance to fire at Larry. Neither could trooper Jackson. The bullets from the guns of trooper Villa, Ralph, and constable Mitch were flying so close that all Bill and trooper Jackson could do was stay down behind their vehicles.

Larry for his part decided to kill Officer Lee. He stepped out from his cover to get in a position to do just that. Gary the sniper and his hunting partner saw their chance. Both fired at the same time. Both bullets struck Larry in the neck. He went limp like a rag doll.

Christy who had been observing this just went silent. She no longer was screaming or making any other noise. She had become comatose, a state from which she would never emerge. Her mind had simply shut down.

Officer Moreland Lee saw his chance. He kicked the back door open and emerged from the vehicle. The thing that saved him was the uniform. All of the combatants recognized the uniform. That factor saved his life. Both snipers had their sights sat on Moreland's chest when one of them recognized the badge and ordered all to cease fire.

Mitch was the first to act. He approached the vehicle with a little caution at first. When he realized that the danger had passed, he signaled the others that all was well.

Officer Lee was overwhelmed at the response he got. One person was asking him if he was okay. Another person was calling for an ambulance. The third officer was talking to his dispatcher. Within minutes an ambulance arrived. A good looking attendant ordered Officer Lee onto a stretcher and began to take his vital signs. He was placed in the back of the ambulance and taken to a nearby Hospital. He was given a clean bill of health. For the first time Officer Lee could move around. His first request was for a telephone to call his wife.

Chapter XVI

The Reunion

Maria had fallen into a shallow slumber aided by a couple of tablets her Bishop had provided. She heard the phone ring but felt that it was another newsman or someone who was nosy and wanted to find out what was happening. Through the exhaustion and fog of the pills, she heard the Bishop answer the phone.

"Lee residence," Stated the Bishop.

"One moment Detective Thomas."

The Bishop turned and handed the phone to Assistant Chief Davis. "It's for you."

Chief Davis took the phone and stated simply,

"This is Chief Davis."

"Yes".

"That is good news. Thank you, Detective Thomas." Chief Davis then hung the phone up. He turned to a subordinate and stated, "wake her up."

Maria was barely asleep when she was shook violently awake by a nearby police Officer. Once she was awake, she sat up on the couch. The first thing she noticed was the officer was grinning. She looked at Chief Davis and the Bishop. Both had smiles on their faces.

Chief Davis in his stoic manner stated, "We have him, he's alive." Maria was too shocked to grasp the meaning of the chief's words.

"I..I..don't..under..understand" she muttered.

She passed out at that point.

www.ingramcontent.com/pod-product-compliance
Lightning Source LLC
LaVergne TN
LVHW041537060526
838200LV00037B/1021